CW01052851

THE SECRE

The Secret Diarists are an anonymous group who have never met and perhaps never will. They came together online and were inspired by one writer's idea to create a collaborative work called The Sheherazade Diaries. Loosely based on the concept of 1001 Arabian Nights, their diverse talents were challenged to create a book of romantic, erotic stories linked by a narrative thread. The aim was to produce sexy, quality writing which would entertain and entice, with the added benefit of anonymity causing no restraint. Inevitably, by the very nature of its uniqueness, the project stumbled and faltered and some members were lost along the way, but the final seven who stayed the course worked hard to embellish, nurture, prune and hack to achieve their goal. With a willing audience, they hope to continue the adventure of anonymous storytelling and they dedicate the work to the inspiration, perspiration and tears of all writers and those who encourage and support them.

www.sheherazadediaries.com

101 Erotic Nights

The Sheherazade Diaries

THE SECRET DIARISTS

Harper*Impulse* an imprint of
HarperCollins*Publishers* Ltd
1 London Bridge Street
London SE1 9GF

www.harpercollins.co.uk

A Paperback Original 2015

First published in Great Britain in ebook format by Harper*Impulse* 2015

A catalogue record for this book is
available from the British Library

ISBN: 9780008140076

Automatically produced by Atomik ePublisher from Easypress

Printed and bound in Great Britain

To those who gave us love, inspiration and helped make this happen … you know who you are. And if you don't, then thank you anyway!

Prologue

What is it with us girls? We try to get what we want, what our hearts desire and sometimes all in the world is just wonderful. We meet the man of our dreams and allow ourselves to be whisked off our feet. We have crushes and days and nights when we simply cannot live without being cradled in his strong arms. We need him. We need him to make love to us with all his strength and passion. We need him to fuck us until our legs are weak and trembling with the effort of taking him in, willingly giving him the same pleasure that we ourselves are taking. We daydream about how it will be happily ever after. We yearn for his total attention and adoration. Sometimes we think that we should have his children, that they will provide a further bond between us, tie us as tight as a wet knot. But then he turns away from us, just a side step at first or maybe the wrong sort of glance at the table and then we glimpse the reality of relationship. That desperate slide into just being there. An inevitable acceptance. The taking for granted. The rare quickie, the occasional after Newsnight and lights out shag that has replaced the slow and considerate mouth watering seduction on the big sofa in front of the fire. It's then we either put up and shut up or if we're like Beth Rogers, we turn to the Sheherazade Diaries to rekindle a hundred and one erotic nights...

"What are you doing, Miles?" I asked.

"Working, darling," he replied, patting me absentmindedly on the arm.

I lay in bed next to him, listening to the tap, tapping of his fingers on the laptop and wondered why things had changed. When did our bedroom become an office? When did it stop being a playground, a palace for lovemaking, touching and talking? A place for intimacy, not the internet?

I moved a tentative foot across the bed and gently stroked his leg, hoping for a sign that the evening could be put to better use.

"I hope you haven't got tired of me" I whispered, waiting for the once inevitable stirring of life beneath my fingers, but Miles sighed and gently pushed me away.

There was a time, only a few weeks ago, when he would have risen strongly at my touch and become hard as teak with a few gentle brushes of my hand.

If it had been a week day we would have kissed goodnight. Even though we were both tired, the kiss would have lingered. Soft and liquid at first, then more urgent. We would have turned to face each other and then Miles would have caressed my neck. I would have slipped my hand down his naked torso until I could feel his arousal. Miles would have gasped with pleasure and then softly rubbed me with his crooked finger. Inevitably we would then have made love. Hard, fast and satisfying. Then, crushed with happy fatigue, we would have slid into contented sleep.

Or if it had been a Saturday morning he might have made love to me for one exquisite hour. Attentive, tender yet full of passion. So loving that I would want to cry with joy.

2

But tonight? Nothing.

"The only thing hard at the moment is the drive on that thing," I said, nodding at the laptop.

"Sorry, darling, got to get this report finished for tomorrow. Maybe later, okay?"

"Oh, right, I'll make an appointment shall I?"

"Don't be like that. I can't help it if sex isn't high on the agenda these days."

"Oh, Miles, I'm not talking about sex. I'm talking about loving contact and passion and wanting each other the way we used to."

"Well, after five years, maybe it's just the way things go."

"But why should it be? On our last anniversary we made love like newlyweds. We said we always would. Remember? That night in the hotel, with the mirror?"

Miles couldn't help but grin. Yes, he remembered.

"You always made me feel that way, Miles. Always. Until the last few weeks, that is."

Finally he shut the lid of his laptop and looked at me properly, "I'm just a bit tired maybe, and stressed … I'm just not as energetic I guess. Don't worry, darling. Everything will be fine. You'll see." He took my hand and guided it down between his legs. The mighty man, once so enthusiastic and inexhaustible, remained stubbornly inert. He sighed and went back to his computer.

If the excitement and spontaneity had gone out of our marriage, it was as much my responsibility as his and I was determined to find a way to restore it. I already had one broken marriage behind me and couldn't watch things disintegrate again. It was heart-breaking. I loved Miles so much and at thirty one, I was also getting broody. There was no way a baby could be a part of our life just now. So, a few days later when Miles was away on a golfing weekend, I went to see my friend Imogen. If anyone could help it would be her.

I've known her for years, since we met on a creative writing course over ten years ago when I was just finishing Uni. We struck up an unlikely friendship; there's twenty years difference in age between us and she was part of my previous life before I met Miles, when I was with Laurent and hung around in quite bohemian circles. So we go back a long way and she has shared many of my ups and downs over the years. I think it's because of this that Miles is not very fond of her.

Imo is quite eccentric, with flamboyant clothes and ever-changing, colourful hair and used to be a theatrical costumier, running her business from a converted granary. Over time, it seemed that her outfits and props were being hired for more than just stage and screen. Sexual role-play became a big thing and customers started asking for somewhere private and discreet to indulge their fantasies. Spotting a gap in the market, Imogen extended and refurbished her premises, providing rooms as well as costumes and toys to suit all tastes and requirements. She also offered personal tuition in the privacy of her 'Playbarn'. Business was booming.

"You need to whet his appetite, Beth. Have you tried dressing up?" she asked me over coffee and cakes, in the comfort of her sitting room.

"Oh yes, Imo. Doctor and nurse, obviously, although Miles found that a bit too close to home once he became a GP! Maid and master … we've done most things in most places over the years. I don't think we've lacked in imagination, it's more as if we've lost that magical, intimate connection we used to have. If Miles isn't working on his computer, he's on the phone or staring at the television. We don't talk properly anymore."

"Well, it's all about communication, isn't it? Have you thought of reading to him in bed?"

"I want to turn him on, not send him to sleep!"

"It all depends on what you read, Beth! You need sexy stuff. Stories, poetry, use the written word to arouse him. What could be more intimate and personal than Miles listening to your voice saying things you know he'd like to hear? I've got a whole library you could borrow!"

"Mmm… sounds interesting."

"That's what Cameron and I used to do. Worked wonders for Anthony and Cleopatra!" Imo wiggled her eyebrows. I smiled at my friend. I had always loved her frankness and sense of humour.

"Listen, here's one of my favourites." She took down an old, tattered book from the shelf and started to read. I was a sucker for old books and still had two first editions that Laurent had given me for my twenty-first.

The story was called *Ghassan* and her warm voice drifted into the air and seeped into my brain.

"That is perfect, Imo."

"Yes, isn't it? And there're lots more besides. You could read him a story every night. See where it takes you."

"Like A Thousand and One Tales!"

"Well not quite, that would be pushing things too far! But look, today's the 22nd of September, why not give it a try until New Year?" Imo counted the days on the calendar. "That's 101 days exactly! Now if that's not an omen, I don't know what is!"

"Imo, that's brilliant! I'm so excited!"

"You should come to the 'Playbarn' and go through all the stuff I've got there, books, magazines and other bits and pieces. There's even a Visitor's Book that makes a pretty good read! See what takes your fancy. I could even ask the folk in my on-line writer's club to come up with something. You're creative Beth, use your skills, change the names, write something yourself. Even Miles might be tempted to put pen to paper. Who knows what you'll come up with?"

I smiled at the thought; why not? I could imagine both of us enjoying it and it would be fun finding things to read to him. If

I couldn't compete with a computer then perhaps I didn't deserve to get my husband back. I would keep a daily journal and fill it with stories.

"Okay, that's what I'm going to do, Imo. You can lend me things to start me off and the rest I'll find in the library or on the internet. You won't mention my name to your club will you?"

"It's all anonymous, Beth. They don't even know who I am!"

The thought took hold and that's how my diary began. Like Sheherazade, I was fighting to change what struck me as a very bleak future and what follows is the uncensored and unabridged account of how I met that challenge. Was I successful? Well, you'll just have to read on to find out.

The Diaries.

Day One – Monday 23rd September.
4.12 pm
Big breath as I start this diary. Putting pen to the pristine pages.
Here goes.

Dear Diary,

Isn't that the way to start off? Haven't kept one since I was
a kid. I went into *Paperchase* at lunchtime and got this
lovely loose-leaf book with natural paper and ribbon
fastening. Must use my best handwriting, so I got a really
nice pen with butterflies on it. I know, I have tons of pens
in the cupboard but I wanted something new and special.

The first story will be easy. It's the one Imo gave me. It's
going to get much more challenging as the nights go on
but fingers crossed that I can keep going.

What's the plan? I'm already a day late in starting; last
night was a washout. Miles came home from the golf
about midnight, pretty drunk and was asleep before I
could even say 'how was your weekend?'

I'm sending him a text asking to meet me at Costa after work. I need somewhere neutral to get his attention and tell him about my idea.

He replied right away.

>>>Sorry love, got to work late home @ 8 xxxxx

Got to work late…

I decided to go to Costa on my own. I needed a coffee. Two lattes. One after the other. Caffeine rush to the head. Sat at the window and watched people go by and wondered where it was all going. Maybe it's me. When I got home I took off all my clothes and looked at myself in the mirror. How many women do this I wonder? The summer tan is still there, a bit. Boobs are lively! They haven't sunk to my navel yet. Miles likes the brownness of my nipples. And my belly's not too round. If I hold myself in it looks quite flat! Legs are still strong, cycling to work helps. No unsightly hair, everything nice and groomed, courtesy of Gina's. Toenails, red. Yet, despite my best efforts, I still feel inadequate somehow. I have Laurent to blame for that I suppose. It's not great for the self-esteem when your husband of 18 months runs off with one of his models. Of course that's what he did with me, and then left his wife. Well, that's another story.

But Miles always loved my body and made me feel good about myself, so there must be something that's turning him away from me.

I can feel this whole idea failing before it even gets going! And I've still to make dinner and have essays to mark for tomorrow. I'll be dead in bed before I can even think about reading Miles a story. But I've really got to try, and my first story is so sweet!

Around 9 pm
"Communication."
"What?" Miles had a mouthful of lasagne.
"I said, communication."

He looked at me and then glanced at his phone for the football results.
"Imo says it's all about communication."
"What is?"
"Our problem."
"What problem? And what's Imo got to do with it?"
"I went over to her house for coffee on Sunday afternoon when you were golfing and we talked about things."

He put down his phone and looked at me with his smokey grey eyes. He frowned and my stomach gave a little lurch as the lines around his eyes creased; he seemed so vulnerable. I felt guilty for discussing our sex life with someone else.
"Why didn't you just talk to me?"
"Oh, Miles. I've been trying for weeks."

I was on the brink of crying and I am almost in tears as I write this now, remembering how hurt he looked. The two of us in the dining room trying to find the right words. I grabbed his hand across the table.
"I love you so much and I want you to be happy. I want you to desire me, Miles."

I find this kind of honest talk quite difficult. My upbringing was of a very down to earth, working class nature, with little room for sentiment and soppy emotions. Sweet talk is embarrassing for me but I had learned some very deep emotions with Laurent and he had taught me how to be naughty. I had never shown this side of myself to Miles. It isn't really me but perhaps it was time for extreme measures. I continued to push the point.

"I am going to be Sheherazade. I am going to read you a story every night for the next 101 days, until the New Year."

He smiled and my stomach lurched again.

"This sounds like one of Imogen's charades. Are you going to dress up like an Arabian princess and do I have to kill you in the morning?" He wasn't taking me seriously.

"I'll dress up if you want me too! And you won't want to kill me because you'll be desperate to hear the next story!"

He leaned over and kissed me softly. I could taste the Chablis on his lips.

"You don't have to go to such lengths, Beth."

"You have to be honest Miles, you've hardly touched me for weeks. I do need to go to such lengths, and I will!"

I showed him the Diary. He could see I was serious.

"Okay, I'll humour you, but I can't see how a story can make any difference."

"Just wait and see."

"Okay, will we finish the wine first?"

11.10 pm

And so we went to bed, a little drunk, Miles smirking at the ridiculousness of it all and me nervous as anything. What if I just embarrassed myself? He made himself comfortable, head back on the pillows, eyes closed. I asked him if he wanted a blindfold and he snorted in disbelief! Silk negligee to the ready, I read the first story.

1. *"Ghassan"*

The 17 year-old Ghassan longed for love – or so he thought. What he really longed for was sex; any kind of sex would do, he just needed an outlet for all this pent up energy, waiting to burst forth and, luckily for him, his cousin Faisal sensed this need. Ever since he was a small boy, Faisal had led the way for his younger cousin and he had watched him these past weeks longingly gazing across the street to catch a glimpse of the college girls before they were whisked away from view. Ghassan's family had big plans for their son, so no early marriage had been talked of; he was to travel to America and attend College there, just as soon as his final year was ended. Meanwhile the urges of a 17 year old boy are strong and, left unfulfilled, begin to take over all his waking hours, and most of his sleeping hours too.
"We have an appointment, Ghassan. Meet me at my market stall around 2pm – and look smart!"
Ghassan was intrigued of course but knew better than to ask questions. Faisal loved a secret and nothing would have persuaded him to impart even a tiny detail of the 'appointment'.
"What is this place, Faisal? Everyone seems to know you."
"All in good time my boy, all in good time."
They sat at low tables and Ghassan was mesmerized by the rustling of the women's skirts skimming the marble floors as they served mint tea in the customary cups. He could feel his usual problem threatening to rear up without much warning, so quickly began a mundane conversation with his cousin about the coming week-end's hunting trip – anything to steer his thoughts away from the bosoms and thighs now so obvious beneath the girls' flimsy attire. Four of them begin to sway to the music and the conversation drifts away to nothing as all eyes are fixed on the gentle movements of the dancers. One of them unties a scarf from her waist and playfully entwines it around Ghassan's neck inviting him to join her and he willingly

11

follows as she leads him through to another room.

A soft, yet firm whisper, "Don't speak", enters his blindfolded world. He knows she's there before the voice confirms it; that unmistakable musky scent combines with an undertone of apricot oil to invade his confused thoughts. The softest touch of a silken finger brushes the downy centre of his abdomen in slow, circular motions moving teasingly downwards. Not sleeping but just below the *surface, inhaling deeply, he is intoxicated by the heady perfume, as a hand slips down to the oily pool that now lies in the well below his belly.*

He hears a murmured inducement: "Lest you wake from your reverie, my sweet boy."

He smells a smoky, woody opiate and willingly sinks into a dreamlike state. Too soft this touch upon his thighs, a tongue tip searches inwards, whilst fingers dip into the oil and find their slippery way to his waiting manhood. Tongue and fingers become one in his dancing mind and still the dance goes on.

Her breath is warm as the Mistral in June as he feels the weight of gossamer-clad breasts fall upon his unsuspecting face. A gasp, "hush!" A throaty whisper from her now as she places a bud-like nipple to his open mouth and he tastes the apricots as she sits astride him:

"Not yet, dear one, not yet …" Her lips so close he feels the breath as she withdraws and slides down to take him in her mouth. A probing tongue lingers and swirls 'til his single thought is of the utter softness of her and he can hold back no longer. Her wet lips graze his cheek in a parting gesture and she gently removes the silken scarf from his eyes:

"Remember me, as I shall remember you, Ghassan." He hears the door click shut. His eyes have yet to adjust but the husky voice and her scent will stay with him always.

11.38 pm
Miles has fallen asleep. I am wide awake. So much for that then!

12

He looks gorgeous lying there, the strong line of his jaw, dark stubble, tousled hair, a bit too long. Is that grey hair at the temples? The moon is bright tonight, waning yet giving a strong light across the room. We sleep with the curtains open – helps us get up in the morning!

I want to draw him. I haven't drawn for ages and my life drawing must be rubbish now. Laurent used to say anyone can draw if they practice enough. He taught me the principles of perspective one hot balmy day in Uzes … enough Beth, enough!

I've fetched my pad and charcoal from the bottom of the wardrobe. Miles is still asleep. I draw his face, every line and crease so familiar and I fall further in love with every stroke. His kind of love, constant, honest.

I'm tired now. It's already tomorrow. I need some sleep.

Day Two – Tuesday 24th September
7.48 am
Miles has woken me with a cup of tea, kissed me on the head and gone off to work. I feel awful. I'm all tangled up in the duvet. My drawing pad is on the floor and there are charcoal marks over the sheets. Did I really draw Miles last night? Haven't lost the skills then. Wonder if he noticed?

Can't be bothered getting up, but must. First class is at 9. They'll be expecting their essays back. The tea is good. Miles knows I like Earl Grey with lemon in the morning. He thinks it's very middle class! I feel so tired … that dream?

Okay, up girl! Short cycle to work will get me going.

10.30 am
Coffee break – starving. Have taken a pastry from the canteen

and am now sitting at my desk. Julie is wondering why I'm not staying to gossip as usual – told her I had work to do. The class were restless today, maybe it's just me. Found the cycle run hard today, seemed uncomfortable! Maybe I need a new seat, maybe one of those soft gel ones for ladies! Don't want to get a thrush infection at this stage in proceedings! Thinking of tonight's story … Maybe I could just read Ghassan again since he fell asleep halfway through.

Text from Miles:

>>>Hi sweetie, sorry I fell asleep last night! Did you have a nice dream? Xxxx

How did he know about my dream …?

12.38 pm
Lunch. No time to write. 'Leaving' lunch for James the technician. He's off on a world trip. Lucky him. Have bored him to death already with tales of my gap year!

5.59 pm
Busy afternoon. Too much paperwork. Home now.

Stripped the bed. Must not use charcoal in bed again! The drawing is good. Make a mental note to do some more.

Imogen's on the phone.
    "How's it going Beth? Did he like *Ghassan*?"
    "Hi Imo! He fell asleep."
    "Early days Beth, early days. Have you got one for tonight?"
    "Maybe!"
    "Okay I'm sending you an email with a PDF of some stuff you might find useful and I've challenged the writer's club to come

up with some stories for you!"

"Okay, that's great, thanks Imo!"

"No probs! See you later. Bye... "

Oh God! It all feels so public somehow. Even though her club is online and anonymous, it still feels like other people are taking over. I'll reserve judgement until I see what transpires but I must find some stuff myself.

What will I do for tonight's story? Last night was a bit disappointing and I can't get the 'dream' out of my head. Did it really happen? If it did, then Miles wasn't so sleepy after all! I'm going to try and scribble it down before he comes home. This will be tonight's offering. I'll call it '2.00 am.' I'll write it from his point of view, that should give him a surprise!

7.35 pm

Managed to write something. Hope he isn't shocked!

He should be home soon. It's his squash night. There's an M&S Jalfrezi in the fridge. I'm sitting watching *Game of Thrones* on Sky eating macaroni and cheese. I'm trying a vegetarian phase. Laurent was vegan. Very challenging. I found Miles such a relief after all of that – he'll eat anything!

8.58 pm

He's still not home. I'm having a cup of camomile tea. Will watch the news.

Ariel Castro has been found dead in his cell. David Cameron on Syria. Mall shooting in Kenya. Depressing stuff.

Thank goodness, I can switch this off – Miles is home!

11.45 pm

I am so embarrassed!

Miles came in. Heated up his meal and sat with me on the sofa. TV went back on. He wanted to hear about the elections in Germany … Arghh… I took out my Kindle and read some poetry, to get ideas. Then I got fed up.

"Do you want to go to bed soon, Miles? I've got another story. I think you'll like it!"

"Sorry that I fell asleep last night Beth, it was very relaxing!"

He pulled me close but continued to watch the News Channel.

"I did have a nice dream by the way."

"What?"

"Your text!"

He had forgotten.

"Busy day. Difficult day."

"Do you want to talk about it?"

"Hmm … better not. Too upsetting, want to forget about it."

"Sometimes it helps to talk."

"You wouldn't like it, Beth. Had to sign a baby into care because his mother had burned his legs with a cigarette."

"Oh Miles."

"And more of the same. Why do people have kids? It's a fuck awful world to bring them into!"

It's so unusual for Miles to swear and he had descended into his 'I don't want any kids' argument which I found hard to deal with. I left him sitting on the sofa and went to bed. I heard him play some jazz on the CD player and knew he would come to bed soon. When he did I held him close and kissed him softly on the lips.

"I wrote this for you Miles, to thank you for last night. It's called '*2 am*'."

2. "2 am"

He could not sleep and looked at the clock, 2 am. He looked across at his wife lying on her back, sleeping peacefully. Her silk chemise had ridden up and he gazed at her beautiful pussy illuminated by the silvery harvest moon.

He moved his head down and planted tiny kisses on her stomach and thighs. Then very gently he parted her legs. He lightly licked her labia, just pushing into her a little. He loved to give cunnilingus to his wife. Not because she might then reciprocate, but because he loved the softness of his tongue and lips against the softness of her clitoris and pussy lips. The closeness and intimacy, the taste and the smell, it was as though he were performing an act of worship to her femaleness.

With his thumb and forefinger he parted her inner lips and darted his tongue against the liquid walls of fleshy softness. With the tip of his tongue he lifted the hood and then licked her clit with slow tender strokes of his rough tongue, exploring her and relishing her smoothness. He stroked his tongue against her a little harder, a little faster. He carried on. Increasing the pressure then barely touching her. Slowing down, then speeding up. He heard his wife moan softly in her sleep and then he tasted the sweet honeydew from her pussy, glistening in the moonlight.

He put his head back on the pillow. It was 2.30. With a sudden rush he felt an overwhelming love for his wife. Then, weary, he drifted into contented sleep.

"Was this your dream, Beth?"

I realised then that he knew nothing about it.

"Did you not do this to me?"

"No. You woke me up, thrashing and moaning."

It was so awful. My cheeks burned red. He looked amused.

17

"Sexy writing though. Sounds like you enjoyed it!"

I was mortified. This is not going the way I planned. Miles didn't seem too bothered; he patted me on the tummy like I was one of his patients, turned over and went to sleep.

So I'm sitting here again writing this in my diary. We are meant to be having exciting sex and I'm turning him off by my stupid stories. I feel so frustrated and foolish. It is pointless. His job is so stressful, I just can't reach him anymore.

Day Three – Wednesday 25th September
7.38 am
The sun is shining, casting a soft light over the bedclothes. I am smiling. Miles woke me with a cup of tea as usual, pulled down the strap of my nightie, lowered his head, hair still wet from the shower and sucked my nipples softly.

"We'll go away for the weekend," he whispered.

I know I did not dream this. Today was going to be better. I pulled off my nightie and lay naked on the bed watching the sun trace across my skin and thought of Miles, and the poem I read last night.

'*Your scent is still on the pillow and I gather the softness into my arms and smell you and the sun comes once more to welcome me through the mottled panes, dancing with lace and comes to rest just for a moment to gather breath, before travelling on a languid journey, taking time, slowly, glancing the tips of my toes and sparkling the hairs on my legs*'.

Oh dear, John Donne will be turning in his grave! But the promise of a weekend away … I wonder what he has in mind?

Back to reality and work. And I need to check my emails and get Imo's stories.

Quick look on the iPad. Yup, Imo's email is there with an attachment. Good! No time to read now. Later. Facebook can wait until lunchtime – I am seriously behind.

10.30 am
Coffee time. Lingered a bit with the office girls listening to the gossip. The new technician is causing a stir. Oh these twenty-somethings – they make me feel so old. By the time I was their age, I had run away with Laurent, got married and was living in the south of France. Seems like a lifetime ago now.

Got an hour to fill before the Rubens lecture. Know this off pat, done it a hundred times – it does make me feel sexy and slim looking at his paintings! If the students knew what was going through my head, haha!

Damn! Damn! Fucking Damn! God I am so angry! Just read Imo's email, quote: … 'By the way Beth, I was in London yesterday to pick up some props and ran into Lucinda, did you know Laurent is staging a retrospective at White Cube gallery next month … Uzes 2003 … Thought you should know …' did she just throw that in for fun? I'm being unkind, she's giving me advance warning, knowing full well how I'll react… but what the hell … he wouldn't dare would he?

12.53 pm
Can't concentrate. Did the lecture on autopilot. Have walked to the park and got a sandwich from Pret. Sitting looking at the ducks splooshing about in the green water. Ripples scattering like my thoughts. He's bound to show the portraits. It's his best work, he always said that. It must be twelve years at least since he had an

19

exhibition in the UK. The press will be all over it. But why Uzes, and why now? I need to phone Lucinda, she'll know more.

"Luce?"

"Beth! Darling, how are you?"

She was just as reassuringly OTT as ever.

"I was expecting you to call. Have you spoken to Imo?"

"What's all this about Laurent?"

"It's true sweetie, I heard it from the horse's mouth myself!"

"What? You've seen Laurent?"

"In Paris, at the weekend. Rob flew me over for a dirty weekend!"

Luce and her lifestyle was one of the reasons I wanted away from London. I couldn't keep up with her. And then there was her penchant for threesomes, which I could not and did not share … So Laurent was still in Paris. Did he still have the studio on Rue St. Jacques where I first met him?

"Oh don't worry babes! At least the exhibition's not coming to Edinburgh until next January!"

Oh God! I don't have that many friends here, and my students are pretty broad-minded but it could be very embarrassing for Miles. Edinburgh was about as far away as we could get. It was an obvious choice for Miles, he did his medic training here and knew the system well. I was a bit reluctant but Imo was here, having moved up with Cameron's job and she convinced me to move to the frozen north. I was really lucky to land the Art History lecturing job at the FE college; it helped that I could name-drop about Laurent Fournier – he did come in useful eventually. And, I have to admit, that in the autumn light, Edinburgh looks stunning today. The artist in me quivers at the beauty of it sometimes…

"There's no need to tell Miles, darling. Why don't you come and stay next month and we can go and see it together … moral support and all that … and you can let your hair down after all those months in that dreary place!"

She had no idea. She thought they all wore kilts, ate haggis and played the bagpipes. When I first told her we were moving, she said 'Oh my God, what will you eat, how will you manage without Waitrose and M&S?'

Well what now? Do I keep it from Miles? Risk upsetting him when he is so fragile?

This calls for serious action. When I'm stressed, I eat. Real food. Miles says I'm only slim these days because I'm happy. I was more Rubenesque, when I was with Laurent, as it will show in the portraits. OMG! Well it could all be about to change – after work I'm going to cycle round to Valvona and Crolla's, see if Giuseppe has truffles, and prosciutto tortellini … Cream … Parmesan … a nice Orvieto Classico … Need to get back to work … And I need another story for tonight … seriously stressed !!!!

5 pm
Managed to get through the afternoon somehow and I've got all the goodies for dinner. Easy to rustle up in a few minutes. Time to download Imo's PDF and see what she's come up with. I'm in need of some TLC tonight. I hope Miles doesn't sense there's something up. I'm almost hyperventilating at the thought of Laurent and the exhibition.

6.15 pm
Well, there's some very juicy stuff in Imo's folder! And much more to come by the sounds of it – quite made me blush and I thought I was a woman of the world. But I'll go easy tonight – don't want to scare him off, haha! There's a lovely one set in Sri Lanka … we went there for our honeymoon so it's quite apt, though we

didn't go for the massage option – wish we had! Come to think of it, there's a box of aromatherapy oils in the bathroom that I got from Lucinda last Xmas …

Writing this quickly before dinner … smells great … Miles is in the shower … He came home with a bunch of pink, sweetheart roses … beautiful... But he was ashen-faced!

"Roses! How lovely, Miles!"

"I've been neglecting you, Beth." He gave me a hug then sat down heavily on the sofa.

"Bad day?"

"The worst."

"What happened?"

"The baby died."

"What baby?"

"The one I told you about. The one with the cigarette burns. I was suspicious about his eye movements and requested a scan. Turned out he'd multiple skull fractures with intracranial bleeding. He started having fits … there was nothing they could do."

"That's awful, Miles."

"The police came to the surgery of course, taking statements. It doesn't look good."

"Why?"

"Well it turns out that Bill had seen the baby the day before and gave the mother a prescription for paracetamol."

Bill was an old-school, misogynist who filled in when they were short-staffed. He must be about seventy.

"And the Health Visitor was in tears."

"Who? Shonagh?"

He nodded. I'd met her at last year's Xmas party. Young, very pretty.

"So what happens now?"

"An inquiry, murder trial, newspapers. The works. After baby P, we'll be dragged over the coals."

"Surely it's not your fault?"

When I first met Miles he was a paediatrician at Guy's. If anybody knew about kids' health, it was him.

"You need a gentle evening, Miles, and I have something in mind that will make you feel better."

I have to concentrate on Miles. My worries about the exhibition will just have to take a back seat. For now.

Midnight
Too tired and full of sex … will write it all up tomorrow!

Day Four – Thursday 26th September
7.30 am
Woken bleary eyed and very tired. The cup of tea on the bedside table is still warm and I vaguely remember Miles kissing me goodbye. He has left a rose on the pillow. How sweet! I feel quite guilty when he has to get up so early.

Last night … The dinner was excellent (I learned a few things from Laurent's housekeeper, Maria. She was a marvellous cook but then I found Laurent was enjoying more than just her culinary skills.) Miles relaxed as the wine and the flavours caressed his mouth. Slowly he began to forget about the horrors of the day and we moved on to the sofa, lit some oriental candles, John Coltrane playing sax softly in the background … And I read him the story.

3. *"Honeymoon Memories"*

We stood on the hotel veranda, enjoying the colours of Sri Lanka, when we were both distracted by movement in the adjacent room. As the verandas were staggered, it was perfectly possible to see almost directly into their bedroom. An Asian couple were entwined in an embrace and as we watched, you

23

drew me close and raised a finger to your lips. The beautiful woman was dressed in a sari of pale lilac and he wore a dark purple velvet jerkin over black trousers. She untucked an edge of the sari and placed it in his palm without taking her eyes from his and slowly she began turning, slender arms raised high, long-fingered hands drawing shapes in the air, the chiffon unravelling as she spun in a passionate, symbolic dance.

In the heat of the afternoon it was hard to tell if our mutual perspiration was due to the temperature or the scene we were witnessing through the patio doors. I could feel your arousal and our breathing became fast as the beauty of the woman was slowly revealed. Her coffee coloured breasts rose and fell, encased in a white lace bodice and she offered them to her man as the finale to the dance was played out. He buried his head in her loveliness and she immediately drew away in a teasing bow of powerful dominance from his pleading, outstretched arms. The second part of her sari was still intact and we both held our breath as she once more began twirling whilst he held the soft fabric and we watched it fall away little by little leaving her long, brown legs exposed. She now stood in a white lace ensemble which he tore away in a show of his own dominance. By then we were wrapped in our own embrace, completely involved in this love-making spectacle.

Tenderness took over and the Asian man laid his naked lady gently down on the rug, entering her with such precision and delicacy, we were moved to sighing. As she reached her climax, we watched enthralled and were frantic to begin our own lovemaking, just as she glanced in our direction and gave a wink – she'd known all along that we were watching.

We walked off the white sand beach hand-in-hand to make our afternoon massage appointment. The room was cool with the sound of the sea crashing on the rocks in the background and views of the turquoise ocean from every aspect. We removed

24

each other's beachwear and stood under a cool shower. As soon as we stepped out we were wrapped in soft white, fleecy towels by a handsome young man in his twenties and a dark-skinned masseuse about the same age. We donned robes and sat in comfy wicker loungers to begin the head massage with almond oil – the boy for me and the girl for you. You reached across and stroked my hand as we drifted in and out of light sleep.

We then lay face down for the body massage and I sensed you were enjoying those delicate yet strong hands easing their way down your spine in slow circular movements. I too felt excited by the firmness of the pressure and the intense aroma of the oils as practised hands moved their way slowly down my legs. At some point – you must have waited until I was completely subdued by the ambience of this relaxing retreat – you quietly took over from my masseur. I felt hands smoothing the inside of my thighs with a greater intensity, teasing that place just below my buttocks. I turned my head to see you naked, your erection sliding easily up and down between my legs, a grin as wide as a Cheshire cat on your beautiful face. You slipped easily inside me and I remember the intensity of us climaxing together with the sound of those crashing waves audible. We sheepishly beat a retreat, running past the giggling masseurs down to the waiting salty sea; I felt happier than ever before in my life and you told me you felt the same.

The following day dawned, beautiful and sun-drenched. We decided to walk and the tree-lined lane offered all the shade you needed to walk and enjoy this remarkable place.

A woman was bent over tending the garden of her little abode and we both breathed in deeply, relishing the scent of rosemary, lemon and thyme, so fresh in the heat. She nodded her head as we passed and beckoned us in, offering a sprig of thyme to me and a hibiscus flower to you, the colour of which was somewhere between apricot and gold:

"Sit in my garden, I bring you mint tea, rest a while."
The smell of incense emanated from the house as she swung
the door and I felt a sense of welcoming peace. We kissed like
teenagers, exploring tongues and teeth in between giggles.
Your hand moved to the flimsy blouse I wore and oh so
gently you pushed against the side of my nipple, back and
forth until I felt the juices flow and the hardness of your
prick against me. As our hostess returned, we straightened
up and took a breath.
"Cooling balm" she said, demonstrating how to rub it lightly
on your neck and wrists. "And mint tea for refreshment."
We offered our thanks, and payment, but she wanted nothing
– "just the joy of watching two young people in love" she smiled
and disappeared inside the bungalow.

I can feel the freshness of the buttery balm now – you began
at my neck and teased each nipple, over and over until I gasped
and thrust your hand 'neath my skirt to rub your creamy-tipped
fingers inside my yielding, fulsome lips. My eyes must have
shown my pleasure because you kissed me with a tenderness I
will never forget and I fell into your arms sated and willing.

… I was wrapped in Miles' arms and he kissed the top of my head.

"That was amazing Beth, I feel as if I'm back there again with
you."

"Come on Miles, I want to give you a massage."

I had no idea how to do it but I was going to try my best.

He laughed but didn't resist as I took his hand and led him
through to the bedroom. Candles still wafted their cinnamon
and ginger vapours and I had draped a beautiful silk sari over
the bed, which shimmered in the dusky light. He let me take off
his clothes, like a child, allowing me to undress him and I laid

26

him down. I spread some oil on my hands and slowly massaged his shoulders, his chest, his stomach, his thighs until he grew beneath my hands. He gave a soft moan and I took him in my mouth. Exhausted, he fell asleep and we lay together most of the night, soundly sleeping.

I feel such a warmth in my belly. The fulfilment of loving him. Storm clouds are gathering and I want to build a wall to protect us from the world outside. I will use these stories to create a little fantasy for us, where we can laugh, love and cry together, and maybe it will help us get through the troubles ahead.

Now ... Enough philosophising – Off to work!

8.15 am
Just about to leave for work. Text from Miles:

>>>"Love you loads xxxxxxxx What's on the menu tonight?"
>>>"Calippos!"
>>>"What??? The ice lollies?? "
>>>"Yup"
>>>"WTF ..."
>>>"Now, now Miles. Don't swear! Love you xxxx"

10.30 am
Pelting with rain this morning. Took the bus. Still feeling warm inside despite the rain dripping down the windows. The whole college feels damp, wet brollies, steaming clothes. Julie got the new technician to check her computer. His name is Alex. It was a bit like a Coke advert, the secretaries all staring at him. At least I was in the office with a credible excuse – trying to sort out the students' assignments, but I found myself smiling at Julie's rather feeble attempts at flirting and thinking about my story for tonight!

Email from Lucinda.

Hi Babes
Re our phone call… Hope you're not too worried about you
know who!
Have to tell more about Paris and Mr X. …

Lucinda has no idea how to be properly discreet – she does all this
cloak and dagger stuff on a private email but posts incriminating
photos on YouTube. Never tell Lucinda anything you don't want
the whole world and his wife to know … I owe her and Imo so
much for looking after me when I left Laurent … they'd warned
me, so had his ex-wife, but they never judged me. Never once did
they say 'I told you so' and they were there for me when I was at
my worst, but they can both be soooo annoying at times!!

She goes on…

Rob and I (and others!!) had a whale of a time and Laurent
was up to his usual shenanigans. He still has the studio you
know, but the stuff he is doing is way over my head, lumps of
paint chucked on canvas if you ask me, darling! Rob wrote a
very graphic account of their doings, to whet my fancy, not
that it needs much whetting Beth, and we both thought you
might like to hear what Laurent was getting up to! So excited
that you are coming to stay … Can't wait!! Have attached
Rob's doc.

Luv Luce xxxx

I do NOT want to read this, but curiosity is getting the better of
me. Not on an empty stomach – Rob's stories are always pretty
graphic! I'll wait until after lunch. Time for class now, Van Dyke…
Wonder where I can buy Calippos?

Lunch

I've just read Rob's account of his jaunt in Paris with Laurent. It's weird, he writes about himself in third person … Luce and Rob obviously write stories to each other about their extra-marital exploits; Imo said she reads stories to Cameron … looks like I've just joined their kinky clique … I'm not sure if I like that!

Miles tolerates Imo and her eccentricities, but he positively dislikes Rob. He thinks Luce is an idiot and a rotten parent, but accepts the fact that I need to go and see them from time to time because I'm the twins' godmother. Best not to think about it too much. Just concentrate on making things as good as I can for Miles. Last night certainly worked and we're both going to need a bit of light relief over the next few months.

Rob's story is not one I could ever read to Miles, but it's par for the course as far as Rob and Laurent are concerned. Seems that nothing really does change … leopards and spots … Laurent was a great lover, no doubt about it. He completely enthralled me, dusky skin the colour of pale gingerbread … he just couldn't stay monogamous … despite purporting to be vegan, his appetite for female flesh was insatiable … and it seems nothing has changed!

4. *"Private Viewing"*

… Apart from the Michelin starred cuisine and service, the best thing about the old restaurant right on the bank of the Seine was its private dining rooms. Each was an exquisite suite with an intimacy all of its own and decorated with style from a bygone age when gentlemen took their female company more seriously than their food. The dark wood-panelled walls had been privy to much debauchery over the years and the four diners that had taken the room on Friday 13th were not going to disappoint. They arrived hot foot from Laurent's private

viewing and even though he had to schmooze with some of the gallery's wealthier clients he had managed several glasses of fizz. Rob too had taken on board his fair share and like a schoolboy let loose in a tuck shop, he had imbibed with enthusiasm. The two girls, Valerie and Chandelle, seemed at first to be taking the art on the walls of Laurent's exhibition a bit too seriously. They arrived and wandered around the show with a distinct air of female Parisian shoppers. Rob thought that even though Chandelle was drop dead gorgeous, she was probably also going to be drop dead dull. Laurent and Valerie had history and Rob could detect the chemistry between the two, that secret invisible cord that trails around between a consenting couple.

"So what dew think?" said Laurent

"I think she looks fantastic," said Rob

"No not her, the exhibition, my latest work, you bastard."

"Oh that. It's up to your usual high standard of bullshit I suppose."

"Well thank you! Thanks a million."

"I guess it will probably earn you about that."

"I wish," said Laurent. "The gallery and my agent will make more than I do on this little lot."

"But you know you couldn't do without them."

The two friends clinked their glasses together before Laurent was ushered away by the flustered French gallery assistant to meet another potential collector. Rob found the two girlfriends standing in front of one of the larger canvasses. It was number 32 and entitled "Candid with a cat."

"Can you see her pussy?" said Rob, who was beginning to feel a bit frivolous after the champagne.

"Wet?" said Valerie.

"Oh I expect so," he said, studying more closely that portion of the painting he thought contained the furry mound covering Candid's crotch.

"Wet, did you say?" said Valerie smiling at the Englishman.

"Oh I see. I'm sorry I misunderstood you. I was wondering if you could see the feline creature alluded to in the picture."

"By veline greeture yer min chat?"

"Yes I suppose I do," said Rob wishing that he spoke better French than he did but loving the sound of Valerie's sexy attempt at English.

"Is there. I sink it ez chat." Chandelle was pointing her perfect finger at a rough patch of thick tortoiseshell-coloured oil obviously applied with a palette knife and given little chance to be stroked by any sort of brush.

"I think you are right," said Rob following the white French finger.

"I am nearly alwizz right," said Chandelle and she recoiled her outstretched digit and let it fall back in place with the others in her hand.

"Is chat," she exclaimed again rather too loudly so that those making their way in procession around the exhibition made a mental note to see if the attractive French girl was right in her judgement of picture number 32.

The fine French bubbles seemed to help to relax the fine French girls. Rob found himself perfectly able to chat to Chandelle and she understood pretty much what he had to say. They found that they had quite a lot in common and there was even something about the French girl that reminded him of the early days with Lucinda. She had the confidence of a woman who knew what she wanted and as the evening progressed Rob knew that Chandelle wanted him.

It was probably Laurent who started the whole thing off by trying to feed Valerie with the asparagus that came with the veal. He picked up one of the butter-dripped spears and held it out, a limp invitation, in front of Valerie's lips and she took it into her mouth in an unhurried, provocative way that told him she was game on. She'd certainly cope with something more

31

enticing than a floppy green vegetable. Spurred on by Valerie's gourmet exhibition, Chandelle picked up her fork and, having speared a portion of meat, she sucked it gently, almost kissing it, before passing it over to Rob making the noise of a French train as she did.

"Choo, choo. Choo, choo!" she said as the fork full made its journey up to and into his open mouth.

"I will," he said. "Every last bit."

With cheese came more fine wine and laughter. Laurent took up his linen napkin and made a blindfold which he tied around Valerie's pretty head so that it looked like a crisp white bandana covering her eyes. Chandelle too had her eyes obscured and the two drunk men started to play the game of guess what it is?

"Is goat shes," said Chandelle as Rob fed her a small portion of soft goat's cheese.

"Bravo!"

"That doesn't taste so good," said Valerie as Laurent put the stem of a carnation into her mouth. Valerie spat it out.

"That's not fair," she complained as he kissed her hard on the lips and pushed some of the wine from his mouth into hers which made her squeal like a schoolgirl.

"Our turn now" said Valerie as she removed her napkin and mopped her chin.

The two men sat at the table in the comfortable chairs with their masks in place. With the dexterity of a skilled undresser Valerie pulled down the shoulder straps to her dress and revealed two beautiful breasts as though it was the most natural thing to do, as though they were a planned part of the culinary experience, firmly on the menu, perfectly and lovingly prepared by a knowledgeable chef. She took the left breast in her hand and encouraged it towards Laurent's waiting and eager mouth. His tongue found the erect nipple before the firm bosom itself smothered his gluttonous mouth. He knew what it was but under his own blindfold Rob could only make out the contented *slurps and grunts coming from his friend.*

"Delicious!" said Laurent when he was allowed to come up for air and he roared with laughter as Valerie put away her assets. Chandelle followed suit and Rob thought that the hard button-like nipple placed into his care was without doubt one of the best puddings he had tasted in a long time.

"I know they are very discreet here but better put a chair against the door," said Laurent as he stood up and dropped his trousers to reveal his stiff artistic intent.

"Oh la la!" said Valerie like a Can-Can girl as she slid onto the end of the table between Laurent and his place.

She sat in front of him with her legs stretched out on each side and without any hint of underwear so that without much difficulty he was able to reach the damp place between her legs with his own upstanding achievement.

"Fuck the coffee!" said Laurent as he placed himself at her disposal.

"Fuck me!" said Valerie as she threw her head back in anticipation of having her request granted.

For a brief moment Rob and Chandelle looked on with mild amusement. What was a bloke to do? But his musings were interrupted when Chandelle dropped to the floor and disappeared under the table. She surfaced moments later in Rob's lap and her nimble fingers, including the one that had pointed so beautifully at Laurent's art, found what they were looking for inside the warm folds of Rob's trousers. Chandelle released the beast and gave a small gasp as she took it into her mouth and sucked and sucked as though she hadn't eaten a thing all day. God, Rob thought, if this is Paris then I'm insane. All four were on the bank of the Seine, in a restaurant, performing as naturally as those that had for generations and they were enjoying the healthy gastronomic feast.

"A very reasonable meal, didn't you think?" said Laurent.

"Thanks for arranging it," said Rob.

"Well thanks for coming, mon ami!"
"Any time," said Rob and the two thumped each other on the back like the naughty conspirators they were.

…This was enough to spoil anybody's appetite! Grabbed a couple of digestives from the biscuit tin and off to enlighten the class with my knowledge of Baroque painting. Taking them over to the National Gallery for an injection of the real thing!

5.26 pm
Home now, students were great. They always love a trip out, especially when it involves a coffee stop! We dallied a bit on the way back to listen to a street busker and one of the girls, Caroline, went off with him to Starbucks. I'm not their keeper after all, and they are adults. He was rather nice looking!

Right. Concentrate! Forget all about today's rubbishy emails. Got a box of Calippos from Sainsburys and they are in the freezer. Also picked up a nice ciabatta from The Artisan Bakery on the corner. It's really a delight living in Stockbridge, and the walk back from town was so lovely, the rain has left everything fresh and glistening.

Turned on the radio to get the local news. Edinburgh City Council is debating whether to renew the licences of certain "massage" parlours in the town … now *that* is funny!

Midnight
Miles is fast asleep

He came home tired as usual but excited.
    "What's all this about Calippos then?"
    "Have you been thinking about this all day, Miles?"
    "Well not all day … had a meeting with Shonagh and Bill about the inquiry. The police have requested that we don't go too

far away over the next few months because we might be called to give evidence, so no jaunts abroad for us then."

"That's a shame, but never mind Miles, I can take you to some fabulous destinations in my stories!"

"Now ... Calippos ... Hope you're not thinking what I'm thinking Beth, you could get an ice burn in a very sensitive place!"

"Well we've got a doctor on hand, but it may not be me who gets the burn, Miles!"

That worried him! We hurried through the meal. The bread was lovely, with some rosemary-infused oil and left-over prosciutto. Dessert was in the freezer! Then on to business! We settled down on the sofa, which seemed to work better than reading in bed (less chance of him falling asleep) some more gentle jazz – didn't want to change the winning formula – and I read the next story which is set in one of our familiar locations.

5. "*Orlando*"

Orlando was 18 and working in the Claims department of an insurance company – hardly an earth shattering job but in these times of recession, he was grateful just to be employed. Rebecca worked in Policies and Orlando spent a good part of his day finding excuses to walk across St James's Square to her department, housed in the opposite building, just to get a glimpse of her shapely legs as she spun round in her swivel chair to acknowledge him. They'd had lunch together in the canteen and when she strode up to order an apple crumble for dessert, he'd been unable to take his eyes off the legs he would very much like to have wrapped around his back, or neck, either would do he mused as she made her way back to sit with him. At 5pm Orlando made sure he bumped into Rebecca as she left the building and boldly suggested they could walk across Green Park together instead of getting the tube at Piccadilly

Circus. It was a real Indian summer and as they walked along in the evening sun, side by side, chatting easily, he was pleased to note he was a good head taller than she was, even in her heels. He was even more pleased when she linked her arm through his, her head resting against him so that he could see the crimson highlights in her dark cropped hair. On a secluded park bench they sat to share an ice lolly, the blackcurrant taste of which was on her lips as he leaned to kiss her in a way he had never kissed a girl before. When Orlando took another bite of the lolly, Rebecca began to lick the juice from his mouth with her delicate pointed tongue and they were lost in an embrace neither of them wanted to end. Rebecca laughed at his obvious hard on and teased him some more with little bites to his ear until he suggested they walk before he ruined the party.

Orlando was in love for the first time and next day sent a text to his love suggesting she might like to try sharing another ice lolly – strawberry perhaps:
"It's a very hot day, tell me how you'd like to share the lolly Lando," she replied.
He loved that she called him Lando but wasn't sure how risqué he could be in his response. In his mind he knew exactly what he'd like to do with a fruit-flavoured ice lolly but he was desperate not to jump the gun:
"I was thinking more of a Calippo, Becky," he ventured, and held his breath.
"Mmmm, sounds delicious, I love ice poles when I'm feeling hot."
Orlando loosened his tie and felt his pants constrict. On previous occasions, he had had a quick fumble with a few of the seasonal temps down in the basement which housed the old 'Bundles'. This was where he sometimes had to go to find some of the really old policies when folk tried to make a claim on a

voided insurance policy. How would Becky feel about meeting him in 'Bundles', he wondered, just as his mobile beeped.
"I'll be in 'Bundles' between 3 and 4pm – make sure you bring the ice pole."
She'd read his mind, this was uncanny, uncanny and brilliant! Just brilliant!

He dug down into the freezer to find the coldest, iciest, straw-berry flavoured Calippo which he prayed wouldn't melt before he made it back to the office. Five to three and Orlando skipped down the three flights of stairs to the basement, slowing at the bottom before nonchalantly whistling his way along the corridor. He could smell her perfume before he caught sight of her sitting on the edge of the enormous wooden table that was used to unfold the old documents. Her lovely legs were crossed and she was leaning back, smiling, waiting for him. This last part he couldn't believe.
She took the ice pole from him and began to stroke it along her thigh. She hitched up her already short skirt and he could see she was knickerless.
"Just watch," she whispered. Rebecca leaned back and slowly pushed the lolly up between the silky curls, just a little way at first and then a bit further as Orlando's eyes struggled to focus. She withdrew the now dripping ice pole and offered it to him to lick whilst he unbuttoned his bulging trousers. She moved closer to the edge of the table and they both licked the lolly, long and hard, their tongues just touching as she guided his hand to her wet, waiting mound. It felt cool and he twirled the hair around his fingers, gently tugging and teasing whilst they demolished the rest of the cold, fruity ice.
Orlando waited as long as he was able before easing his cock between her cool, gaping lips and those long-desired legs wrapped themselves around him. The taste of Rebecca and the strawberry ice mingled and he lifted her from the table, her

37

arms around his neck, so that he could reach further inside
and give her all of him. She drew away just at the end so that
she could watch his smiling face as they cried out in unison.
'Bundles' would always hold a special place in both their hearts.

…. What can I say? We did exactly what it said on the tin! Except they were Tropical flavoured Calippos, not Strawberry!!

Miles went to bed with a big grin on his face and I think he managed to forget about the problems at work. And we have our weekend away to look forward to … so far so good …

Day Five – Friday 27th September
8.05 am
Friday! I was up first for a change and gave Miles tea in bed. He was all tousle-haired and sleepy.

"Where are we going tonight?"

"Not telling! My turn to give you a surprise!"

I wondered what he had in mind. I kissed him on the cheek and snuggled down beside him until it was time for him to get up.

The memory of last night is still tasting sweet on my lips! But I need to tell him soon about my plans to go to London. It will spoil things, I just know it will. Maybe there'll be a time at the weekend when I can break it gently.

Laurent is not going to go away. I need to find out if he is planning to show the portraits. I tried to destroy them before I left Uzes, after the huge row – threw paint thinner over one of the bigger canvases – but Laurent just laughed. He promised he would never show them publicly, so why now, after ten years? He can't need the money, surely?

Will cycle to work today, the sun is shining. Try to find a happy thought … Think of Calippos …

10.30 am

Coffee time. Had an easy morning, debriefing the class about yesterday's visit to the gallery. Noticed Caroline had a dreamy look on her face – maybe her coffee with the busker led to better things!

Julie has managed to get a date with Alex the technician, much to the annoyance of the secretaries. She will give us all a blow by blow account on Monday morning no doubt. She knows Miles is taking me away for the weekend and has been nudging and winking, "Clock's ticking, Beth!" I hate to tell her that Miles doesn't want kids. It was something we agreed before we got married and it's not up for discussion. But I seriously hope that I can change his mind. If I'm honest with myself, that's one of the reasons behind the diary, hoping … and wishing…

It's rather ironic that Laurent, who would have been a terrible father, was dead keen to start a family and was devastated when we lost the baby. I cried of course, but in retrospect it was for the best. He went right off the rails. Two weeks solid drinking. He said it was my fault, as he would. That was the final nail in the coffin for me.

Cheer up Beth! Time for the Rococo … I'm certainly rattling through the centuries!

12.58 pm

Out for lunch. Sandwich from Pret. Hummus and sun-dried tomatoes on sour dough. Watching the ducks again. I'm beginning to recognise them. There's a frisky brown and white one who manages to bully his way to get the crumbs. I have taken to sketching on the margins of the diary and little duck is there – I'm going to call him Freddy – I have gone all Beatrix Potter!

Just beyond the pond, I can see Caroline sitting on the grass having lunch with her busker friend. They look quite cosy together, so it wasn't just a one-night stand then? I wonder what it would be like to just pick someone up like that? Once you're married, that spontaneity just goes out the window but I suppose you could imagine a scenario, just for fun?

6. *"One Hit Wonder"*

There was this guy standing in the derelict doorway strumming his heart out on his twelve-string and singing with such conviction, that I did a double take. Normally in Rose Street I hurry straight past the performers. Their mediocrity doesn't prompt a sideways glance. But this guy was different. He was good. Better than good and, corny though it sounds, he stopped me in my tracks. I guess it was his voice more than his strumming. It was a cross between Michael Bublé, Bono and that young Scottish lad who got to the final of X factor. I know. It's a difficult one to pigeon-hole or imagine but trust me, he sang like he meant it. I guess that's it. Every note and every word was filled with a passion that you'd expect from a fully-fledged opera. So rather than just stop, listen for a while, find some coins or even a note to drop in his open guitar case and move on, what did I do? I stood there gawping like some schoolgirl groupie and when he had finished his song I clapped.

 "Bravo!"

"That was beautiful!" I said. "Would you like to come and have a cup of coffee with me?"   And he said "Yes please, that would be nice." So we went into Starbucks and I bought him an Americano and I had a skinny latte and we sat there as though we had known each other for ages. We talked about music and singers and songs and performers and groups and venues and he was interesting and interested. And when he had finished his coffees (he had two) he said "It's really nice to meet you and I'd really like to see you

40

again." And instead of saying "Well it was good to meet you.
Best of luck with your music and I'm sure you'll do well.
I'm very busy, happily married so I don't think it would be
appropriate to meet up again," I heard myself saying "Yes
that would be great." And that was how I met my strolling
minstrel, as I called him. We arranged to meet the following
Wednesday afternoon when I knew that I would be free and
he took me back to his room. I felt like a teenager all over
again. His grotty room was up so many stairs in one of
those big run-down Georgian buildings filled with University
students. He made me mint tea and played gentle songs to
me on his guitar and it seemed the most natural thing in
the world to make love. We did, my strolling minstrel and
me. We made love in his cramped bed with a poster of John
and Yoko watching us. It was wonderful, unexpected,
impromptu, on-the-spur-of-the-moment, reckless, naughty
(very naughty), unnecessary, out-of-order and wonderful.
Would I do it again? No. I don't need to do it again. He
was my one hit wonder.

Haha! So much for daydreams! Quite a fun way to pass a lunch
hour though. Wonder if Miles does this? Must ask him.

Right, back to the fray – short afternoon and then quick cycle
home. Can't wait to find out where Miles is taking me!

6.38 pm
Miles is in the shower. We had a quick cup of tea before getting
ready for the mystery outing!
    "Do you ever daydream about having sex with somebody else?"
    "All the time!"
    "What?"
    "It's a male thing Beth! They say most average males think
about sex every ten minutes, and not only with their wives!"

41

"You just made that up!"

"No, it's true!" He laughed. "You would not want to hear the conversation in the clubhouse!"

"Oohh … Tell me more…"

"That would be breaking confidence, Beth!"

I hit him round the head with the tea towel.

"Tell just a teeny one… "

"Well one guy fantasises about Russian prostitutes and an old bloke and his wife go to swingers' parties."

"Really?" I hesitated … "I had a sexy daydream today" … Miles raised his eyebrows …

"I wrote it down. I imagined picking up a busker in Rose Street and making love in a grotty student flat in Marchmont!"

"Sounds more like a nightmare Beth, if it was anything like my student flat!"

"I did do some sketching as well, ducks in the park." Just to let him see I wasn't totally obsessed with sex!

"You've got too much time on your hands! But I'm really pleased you've started drawing again. This diary of yours is giving you a lot of fun."

What he said was true. Everything seems more alive and 'real' somehow since I started writing. The diary is becoming more than just a collection of sexy stories to stimulate Miles, it's making me think about my life, my past, my future and it's giving a focus to my day. It's like having a bosom friend to confide my secrets. I realise now that with Miles working so hard, I have actually become quite lonely.

"So, are you going to tell me where we're going?"

"Wait and see!"

Miles drove out of the city and after a while I realised where he was taking me, Dalbinnie House Hotel, just outside Glasgow. The one with the mirror!

7. "Hotel Love"

We checked into the hotel and went to our room.

"The bed's high," I said, thinking it would be difficult to climb in.

"Looks perfect," you said. You were considering the height in a different context.

"So" I said brightly "what shall we do? Book dinner? See what's on at the theatre?"

You don't answer but walk over and embrace me. You kiss me hard. I should be angry with you, but it's not possible.

You undo your trousers and let them slip off, then pull down your pants and kick them off.

I look down. You are flaccid, a little firm perhaps. But as I look, you rise up like a crane. I stroke you with one downward movement and then give a little pinch at the bottom of your scrotum. You gasp. Moving my hand back up, I feel your balls tight as walnuts and you are now vertical and very hard.

You remove my skirt and start to stroke my inner thigh with your index and second finger. Pulling aside my knickers a little you stroke my lips. You slide both fingers in, only a little way, and make a circular motion inside me. Now I want you completely. I take off my knickers. You look down and give little gasps of admiration as you always do when you see me aroused. You kiss me again. Passionate, hard, long. Then you turn me around and push me down onto the bed.

You're right. The bed is the perfect height. It comes to my waist, so I can bend over at ninety degrees. I'm face down on the bed, but you are able to spread my legs just enough for you to slip inside me, hot and wet and making a slight squishing sound. You push your thighs forward and thrust right inside me. Then you move back and pull right out so that when you push back the head rubs against my labia. It is exquisite. And you carry on like this moving in and then right out and in again.

You're making love to me, harder and harder making me pant with joy. I love it when you take me from behind, the only downside being that I can't see your beautiful face.

Then something miraculous happens.

"Look up, Beth" you say.

I look up and I'm looking at you. The full length mirror above the bed. I look at your face as you make love to me with greater and greater intensity. You smile at me. I smile at you. You're holding me by the hips thrusting your large cock in and out of my pussy, your thighs slapping against my buttocks. Lovemaking cannot get any better.

But then it does. You lift my left leg onto the bed, bending at the knee. This causes me to open a little more and rubs my clit against the end of the bed.

"Oh my God, that feels divine" I gasp.

"Oh my God, that looks divine" you gasp as you can see me open for you, red and yearning.

As I come, I ejaculate a little onto the floor, but I don't care. You lightly spank my right buttock a few times and then come inside me. Strongly, deeply, gloriously.

You lean forward, fatigued, and kiss the back of my neck. Then you straighten and lift my head gently. You look at my face in the mirror and smile.

As you catch your breath you say "Oh God, I love you, Beth."

"I love you too, Miles."

We never did make it down for dinner. Afterwards, we were so hungry we had to order room service!

Day Six – Saturday 28th September
9.12 am
I have slept late, in this big comfy bed. I can see my sleepy head in the mirror above and think of last night.

44

Miles has gone. Left a note on my pillow, 'Off to the Gym. Will bring back breakfast xxx.'

I have a few more minutes to snooze.

Ping! Email. Imogen

> *Hi Beth*
>
> *Hope all is going well! Don't mean to intrude on your lovely weekend but thought you might need some more stories.*
>
> *Lucinda tells me you are going down to London next week … Please be careful, you know how persuasive Laurent can be.*
>
> *Have fun*
>
> *Love Imo xx*

Does she think I can still be beguiled by Laurent's charms? As if!

She has attached another folder of stories. At a quick glance, it looks as if she knows some of Miles' golfing chums!

Midday
Miles came back armed with a tray groaning with croissants, coffee, toast, jam, butter, porridge, honey, cream … we sat in bed, Miles still damp from the shower.
    "Did you have a good workout?"
    "Mmmm …" with a mouthful of toast … "need to keep my fitness up for next month's hill-walk."

He goes away three times a year with his Uni pals, The Extreme Medics. Nepal, Mont Blanc, Apennines … next up were the Cuillins in Skye. I had been there once, camping. No climbing for me.

"What's the plan for today?"

"Thought we could just stay in bed, Beth!"

Now it was my turn to refuse.

"I'm sore!!! Give me a couple of hours to recover!"

He laughed and switched on the TV.

… £9m action plan for A&E as winter crisis looms, Inspector tells GPs to improve their services or face closure, £400 million for new cancer drugs … Miles moaned and switched it off.

I gave him a hug. I could feel the muscles under his tee shirt.

"Men are so hard!"

"I thought that was the point, Beth!"

I punched him in the ribs. "Not that, idiot! It's just that you get me, all squishy and soft and smooth, and I get you, all hairy and tough!"

"Mmmm see your point," as he took another bite of croissant… "I've no answer to that Beth, unless you want to try lesbian sex. Can't help you there." I gave him another punch.

"I had a crush on a girl once, when I was at school. Never did anything though."

"Another of your fantasies, Beth?"

"Talking of fantasies, I think Imo knows some of your golfing friends, by the look of her recent stories!"

He was not amused and poured himself some more coffee.

"While you're munching away, I'm going to read you a story about a girl on a bus. This one's for me, nice and soft!"

8. *"The Girl on the Bus"*

Sometimes you're running late. I like those times best, when your cheeks are flushed like peaches and my stomach lurches and my heart beats, beats, beats until I can barely contain a groan.

Today, you sat right in front of me and I stared at your neck, wisps of hair falling loose from the jewelled clasp and tendrils dancing about your skin, auburn freckles and hints of blonde where the sun has kissed you and I see a bead of sweat, dripping so slowly, slowly, that I want to place my tongue and taste the salt.

If I look at your sandaled feet, I am lost. You keep changing the colour of your nail-varnish, just to tease me. When it is blood red, I feel such an intense longing for deep passionate kisses, on a rug by a roaring fire, with oozings of mouth and wetness between my legs and dark skin shining in the light of the flames and it makes me swoon in agony.

And some days your toes are pale, pastel pink and you are soft and floaty and I dream of a beach with rolling waves, frothing and lapping and we laugh and giggle, our brown skin naked in the cool sparkling sea, and you tickle and rub and put your fingers inside me and round and round pushing and rubbing until you make me come, wild and frantic, pulling me down in the water until we fall exhausted and spent, on to the boiling hot sand. And we lay together, breasts on breasts, breathing in time to the rolling tide and I bury my face in your sweet smelling hair, and take your nipple in my mouth so comforting, like a baby feeding and I feel the curve of smooth skin under your arms like the silk inside of an oyster shell. And then the sweet, salty smell and taste of you, like the warm summer sea and a mound of soft hair that caresses a clitoris, which bursts to life on my tongue. Then, finally and most wonderfully, a wet moist tunnel that beckons me in, secure and tight.

And one warm day in spring, you drove me frantic, in a green
dress with yellow flowers and I dreamt of making love to you
in the grass, with wind in your hair and butterflies skipping
overhead as I licked your nipples until they were scarlet and
maybe someone is peeping over the hedge and we are excited
at the thought of being caught and how I dread the winter
when you will wear shoes and boots and jackets and coats and
I will no longer see your toes.

"It is like that Beth, warm and soft," and he nibbled my ear
and kissed my neck.

We cuddled for a while, eating the last of the breakfast and feeling
so stuffed with food, it was an effort to do anything.
    "Did you have any plans for today?"
    "I've got tickets for the opera tonight."
    "Which one?"
    "Queen of Spades."

That's a new one for me. Miles is watching Sky Sports and I have
just finished writing … We have been lying in bed all morning!
It is well into the afternoon and I am getting up, now!

6.09 pm
Trouble! Very upset. Have had to lie to Miles. Not good.

We have always been very honest with each other. He knows all
about my gap year, the time in Paris, Laurent, the pregnancy.
Equally I know all about his student exploits, his six year tryst
with Judith, a German linguist. We gelled because we had both
emerged from long, damaging relationships and we promised
ourselves honesty. Before today, I have only lied to Miles twice.
And now … how lies beget lies.

48

I came out of the shower, wrapped in a fluffy white bathrobe and had intended giving Miles a quickie before we got ready to go out.

I could see the expression on his face. More hurt than angry. He was holding his phone.

"When were you going to tell me?"

I felt my stomach clench and my heart started racing.

"Tell you what?" I stuttered.

"That you're going to London next week. To see Lucinda."

Relief. *That*, I could blag about. Laurent, I could not.

"How do you know about that?"

"Lucilubes has posted it on Facebook." He reads his phone, "I quote, 'my gorgeous friend Beth is coming to stay next week. What fun!' unquote."

Lucinda!!

"You know what she's like Miles. You've said yourself, anyone who give themselves the moniker lucilubes69 is an idiot!" I tried to diffuse the situation.

"Are you or are you not?"

"Am I or am I not what?" I was beginning to get annoyed with his attitude.

"For God's sake Beth, stop being disingenuous! You know full well what I mean!"

"Yes, I was planning to go and visit." The lies started to pile up thick and fast. "I meant to tell you but it went out of my mind. I promised ages ago to go down and see the twins on their next break from school."

"It's not half term yet. And anyway, Lucinda usually packs them off to her mother's for the holidays."

"There's some special Founder's Day holiday or something and she's already told them I'm coming. I am their godmother after all!"

49

They say the best line of defence is attack and I was hitting below the belt. I'm not proud of this. Anything to do with the twins would always win him over. He knew how Lucinda and Rob had little time for them and how much they looked forward to my visits. His own experience of boarding school made him only too well aware of their situation. But I was using them to cover up my deceit. Of course they would not be there.

"I just wish you had told me." He was defeated and my heart was aching for him.

"When are you planning to leave?"

"Oh it's up to Luce." I tried to sound casual and it came across as flippant. "Maybe Wednesday or Thursday. The students have a reading week so it doesn't really matter."

His face was grey. "The inquiry is being held on Friday. I really hoped you would be there for me."

I can't even begin to explain how this made me feel. He needed me and I was deserting him. All my efforts to stimulate our marriage had been erased in one second. Yet I had no choice. Bigger things were at stake but I couldn't tell him the truth. I just had to watch the hurt and disappointment turn to placid resignation.

"Best get ready to leave. Curtain's up at 7.30 and it takes twenty minutes to get there."

He is in the shower and I am trying to stop myself from crying. The little black dress is mocking me and I can barely bring myself to put on make-up.

Day Seven – Sunday 29th September
1.30 am
Wide awake. It's already tomorrow. Miles is fast asleep, face down, exhausted.

The evening went slowly and with minimal conversation. We drove the short journey in silence, the sharp lights of the traffic spiking into my eyes from the darkness.

The theatre was busy. Everyone dressed to the nines. I saw someone with tiara and furs, there were a few kilts and some students vying for stand-by seats. Miles had bought expensive ones – front row Dress Circle. I read the programme to get up to speed on the plot. Pretty grim stuff and I knew I would cry. Miles was very sweet which made me feel even worse. I forced myself to eat an ice cream at the interval so he wouldn't see how upset I was. I always have an ice cream. I burst into tears when Lisa flung herself to her death and when Gherman killed himself, the shot of the pistol made me jump in my seat.

"I've never seen you so moved by an opera, Beth."

I couldn't answer.

"Do you want to grab some food before going back to the hotel?"

"No. Can we just get room service again? Couldn't face a restaurant."

Miles tried to keep the conversation going on the drive back and I forced myself to respond. By the time we got to the hotel I was feeling angry; angry with Laurent for putting me in this position and found myself wanting to take it out on Miles. So when he asked if I fancied a game of strip poker, I said yes. One of the lies I had told Miles was that I was hopeless at cards. I nearly always let him win, having just the occasional success to make it look more normal. In fact, I am a very good poker player. My years with Laurent – who is a consummate cheat – had taught me some very useful skills. I was determined to win tonight. The opera had given me an appetite for a game.

9. "Strip Poker"

We went to see 'The Queen of Spades' and when we got back, we both wanted the evening to continue. Miles suggested a game of strip poker. A game of strip poker with a difference. Whoever was the loser, that is whoever was naked first, had to give pleasure to the winner. The loser could only give, not take.

It was a cold autumn night so you lit the fire in the huge fireplace that dominated our hotel suite, light flickering across walls and reflecting off the mirror. You opened a bottle of wine and played some Miles Davies on the CD player. The sinuous trumpet weaved round the throbbing bass, augmented by little splashes of piano. Funny, I didn't really get this sort of music at first, but it's grown on me over the years.

We both sat on the oak floor in front of the fire, two steaming goblets on the hearth. You opened the fresh pack of cards that you got from reception, and shuffled. I cut the cards and you dealt the hands.

First hand you won, so I took off a shoe.

I won the next one and you took off a shoe.

For the first few hands the game was pretty even but then you started to win. After a while I was wearing just my black bra and panties while you were still wearing your trousers and both socks.

You dealt the next hand. I had two eights, two fives and a two. I discarded the two and drew another card. A seven. Two pairs. Not bad I thought, until you turned over your cards. Three tens. You won again.

You didn't say anything, just made a gesture with your hand. I slid off my panties and sat with my legs parted a little. The wood floor felt cool on my bottom. We smiled at each other and then you lowered your eyes and gave a little gasp as you caught a glimpse of my pussy.

You picked up the cards and shuffled them, a little smugly I thought, as if you knew the game was yours. I knew if you won this hand I'd have to take off my bra and then do whatever you wanted me to, for your pleasure. I wouldn't mind that too much. I love giving you pleasure and I know you feel the same, but tonight I wanted to win.

I picked up my cards. Awful hand. A pair of nines. I drew three more cards but it didn't help. I was left with a pair of nines. I was reaching round to undo my bra straps when you turned over your cards. A pair of fours. I won. You removed a sock.

I won the next hand too, and the next. You took off your trousers and sat wearing nothing but boxers. Tight black boxers. With a telltale bulge.

So it all came down to this hand. You dealt the cards. You looked through your hand and smiled. I had nothing. A queen, a ten, a nine, a four and a two. In desperation I kept the queen and drew four cards. You drew none and you couldn't hide a little smile of triumph. By some miracle, I drew three more queens and a jack.

"There you go, Beth. Full house. Kings and tens," *you said triumphantly.*

"Sorry, Miles. Four queens. And a jack."

"What? Four queens?"

"That's right, Miles. And a jack. And queens finish on top of kings. So your jack there in your boxers gets nothing tonight."

"Well played, darling," *you said. You stood up and slowly slid down your boxers. Your cock looked magnificent. Large, smooth, proudly erect. You turned and I watched you go and fetch another bottle of wine. I always enjoy looking at your tight arse. You came back with the jug and poured us each another goblet.*

"Now, Miles. It's all about my pleasure tonight. You get nothing.

Okay?"

"Of course. You won. So, what is your pleasure, my darling?"

"Lie down on the floor. On your back."

You lay on the carpet, naked. I got on all fours and slowly positioned myself just above your mouth. I was facing your feet so that I could see your naked body.

"Put your tongue out, but don't move it. Down, as if you're licking your chin"

You put your tongue out and extended it downwards. I lowered myself so that it was just touching my clitoris. As I slowly rocked back and forth, the upper part of your tongue rubbed against my clit. It was rough like sandpaper. Rough but exquisite, and as I pressed myself against it great waves of pleasure surged through my body.

I leant forward and very gently stroked your scrotum. Your balls were hard and tightly flattened. Then with a finger I drew a line from your balls up your shaft. You trembled then gasped with pleasure.

I sucked on my fingers for lubrication, then slid my hand down, lightly brushed your balls and moved further down over the perineum and slipped my middle finger a little way up your arse. I bent it back and forth and then pushed it further.

"Now remember, Miles, this is about my pleasure, not yours."

So I carried on rocking back and forth. I moved forward a little so that your tongue pressed against my labia and pushed inside my pussy, as much or as little as I wanted. At the same time I was pressing my clit hard against your mouth. I was fully in control and could enhance the pleasure by moving my body back or forward.

I could see your hands move towards your cock, so I pushed them away. No pleasure for him tonight. I could see your muscles spasm making it jerk up and down a little.

I know how much you love cunnilingus, pleasuring me, darting your tongue in and out of my pussy, lapping hungrily at me, enjoying the taste of me. Now I was rubbing myself against your tongue faster and faster and was pressing my clit down with more and more force.

I could feel myself coming and bent forward so that my mouth was inches from your erection. I put my lips around the head and sucked, lightly, once or twice. Then a marvellous orgasm rushed through me and I collapsed on top of you. You were gasping for breath, your mouth covered in my love juices.

"Thank you, darling" I panted.

You were still trying to catch your breath.

"You're delicious, Beth. I just wish I could breathe through my ears," you said, finally.

I could see that you were aching for me, but I didn't allow you any other pleasure.

8.12 am

Splitting headache. I can see the remnants of last night on the hearth, two empty bottles of Rioja, my black underwear and the pack of cards splayed across the wooden floor. The sun is biting into my eyes, making me feel sick. Can barely hold the pen. Miles has gone to the gym again. I must get some paracetamol and a cold flannel for my head.

6.12 pm

Sunday has passed in a blur. Miles brought me some breakfast but I couldn't touch a thing. He thought it was funny seeing me with such a hangover and insisted on feeding me warm porridge. Rob's story came to mind as I sat there, blindfolded by the flannel and Miles feeding me. Not a pleasant thought.

Somehow I managed to get showered and dressed and we checked out about eleven. I suppose the weekend has been a success, but the outcome wasn't quite what I had expected. Miles is on a high and I'm in the doldrums. He has totally forgiven me about going to Lucinda's which makes me feel even worse. I am hiding behind my headache.

Miles is on his laptop in the dining room table writing up a report for Thursday's inquiry.

I am sitting in bed with a mug of ginger tea which Miles kindly made for me. I need to text Luce and arrange a flight.

>>>Hi Luce How's it going? When do you expect me down? Just about to book my flight, Love Beth xx

She texted back immediately

>>>Hi Babes how goes? Can't wait to see you!!!! Any time on Wednesday would be perfect. Seeing my therapist first thing, but can pick you up any time after lunch. Let me get your flight sweetie – got tons of airmiles darling, don't take those dreadful bucket airlines… (even Business Class is roughing it for Luce – Rob's a pilot with British Airways)… Jules will drive us… (Rob's driver… Luce has him for breakfast!) … and we'll have afternoon tea at The Ritz, the Maître d' owes me a big favour! Luce xxxxx

For all Lucinda's faults, no-one can accuse her of being ungenerous! Part of me was looking forward to seeing her. Life with Luce is never dull and luxury comes as standard. First Class flights and tea at The Ritz – I could cope with that! Makes things a bit better I have to say.

Miles is still hunched over his lap top. I'll go and see if he wants a cup of tea. Feeling much better now.

7.35 pm
Lovely smell coming from the kitchen. Miles is making dinner – says he needs the distraction. He struggled today with the report and wanted to speak about it.
    "I know I did everything according to the book, but Bill and

56

Shonagh are finding it hard to justify their actions."

"That's nothing to do with you is it? As long as you're okay?"

"Not as simple as that Beth. The whole GP Practice is under scrutiny and the media will have a field day. We missed several opportunities and failed. Somebody should have stepped in and saved the poor mite. Social Work are going to come off badly as well. It's not looking good."

"But surely it's the parents' fault. They're the ones who failed!"

"Duty of care and all that Beth. It's a murder inquiry now. They've charged the boyfriend."

In some ways I'm glad to be going away. It could all get quite depressing. Might actually be best for Miles if I'm not here. I have very strong views on this, and it brings up bad memories for me.

I'm sitting on the sofa scribbling, in between reading the Sunday papers. I see Bridget Jones is back! Diaries r' us!! But sad news … Darcy is dead … for goodness sake! That's awful. No more Reindeer jumpers.

11.30 pm
Miles is asleep.

He made a superb risotto for dinner, just the right amount of creaminess and lashings of Parmesan. A teeny weeny glass of Orvieto for me. Miles showed great restraint on the alcohol as well!

We cosied up on the sofa and watched Bridget Jones' Diary in homage to Darcy. Not really Miles' cup of tea but he was glad of a little light relief!

"Christmas jumpers are going to be de rigueur this year, Miles!"

"Don't even think about it Beth!"

When it came to bedtime, Miles asked for a story! Something

funny he said, to keep the mood going. I thought of Lucinda and her therapist. Now that would be funny, to be a fly on the wall! One of Imo's stories was on a similar theme.

In bed, cuddled up in Miles' arms I read …

10. *"Leonard and Angela's First Hypnotherapy Session"*

"Today, Angela, I want you to completely relax and tell me when you feel you could float away. Then I want you to go back to when you think these 'fantasy' episodes first began."
"Yes, Mr Laleham, it usually takes a few moments, but now, yes now, I am relaxed and floating."
"Good, now how old were you Angela, when you first remember fantasising about sexual encounters with …, well, you tell me, and I'll sit back and listen."
"When I was 17, we had a neighbour, not next door but three doors away, Don Lambert. He was an insurance salesman and I knew that every time I walked down the communal pathway, well it seemed like every time, he would be there watching me. The thing was, I liked it. I liked it a lot. So I started wearing shorter skirts, tighter blouses and making sure he had a good view as I walked by. Then as soon as I got indoors, I'd run upstairs to my bedroom, it was at the back and overlooked all the gardens, open the window and lean out with all the buttons of my blouse undone. He was always there, ready for me, pretending he was gardening or taking the rubbish out, just waiting for me to show him my tits. I could see the bulge in his trousers as I bounced them up and down a bit and then I'd lean a bit further forward as he rubbed himself off with a hand in his pocket. When he went back indoors, I'd lay on my bed and think of all the different ways I could arrange to be alone with Mr Lambert. I could imagine us in his garden shed – I'd pretend dad wanted to borrow his garden rake or

something, in his garage – I'd knock on the door and ask if he could help me fix a puncture on my bike. That was my favourite fantasy because he'd offer to adjust my saddle for me if it was uncomfortable for me to ride. Then he'd explain that I needed to get used to the feel of it between my legs and that there was a good way to practise if I liked. I'd notice his cock sticking out under his overall and he would tell me to stand on tip-toe, like I was getting on my bike, and to ease myself back onto him and slide back and forth, just like it was a saddle."

"So, Angela, nothing ever happened between this Mr Lambert and yourself, these were pure fantasies?"

"Apart from the show at the back window, yes, that was it."

"Next was the old chap from the driving school who would pick me up twice a week for lessons. He was old, 45, maybe and when we were actually driving along in the car, I never gave him a second thought. It was later, when I was alone, I began to invent little scenes in my head."

Leonard realised he was looking forward to hearing what Angela had to say next, rather than sitting there idly doodling in his pad, he was leaning forward, admiring the rise and fall of her flat tummy, the hardness of her nipples visible through the pastel pink of her dress and the slight shimmer of perspiration above her distinctive cupid's bow. Her chestnut hair framed the heart-shaped face perfectly, the 'widow's peak' adding an air of the exotic to her olive-toned skin. Normally so professional in his approach, Leonard found himself flustered and a little breathless, relieved that Angela was under hypnosis and couldn't see his now obvious hard-on.

"Tell me about the driving instructor fantasy, Angela."

"Mr Saward is in the passenger seat, quietly giving me directions when he reaches across to suggest that his hand on my leg might help to steady my nerves. He gently strokes the inside of my thigh, slowly moving his hand higher and deliberately

59

pushing my skirt up at the same time. I carry on driving as if nothing is happening but I'm getting very wet and by the time his hand brushes between my legs he can feel the dampness and I part my legs so that he knows what I want."

Leonard interrupts her flow to ask "and what is it that you want at this point, Angela?"

"I want him to tell me to stop the car and to climb into the back seat, lift my skirt, take my knickers down and let him spank me, telling me how naughty I am to have encouraged him. He then tells me that I need a proper seeing to so he's going to take me to the barn in the village and show me exactly how I should be punished. We drive to the barn and he tells me to go on ahead of him, so that I'm leaning across the hay bale with just my underwear on, waiting."

At this point, Leonard lets out an involuntary moan of ecstasy at the thought of this young girl in white cotton briefs and matching bra; he coughs and tells his patient to continue.

"Well when I take my dress off, I can't wait for Mr Saward to appear, I'm so turned on, so I start to rub my clit with my fingers as I'm leaning over the rough straw bale. When he arrives, he chastises me for what I'm doing and begins spanking me with a flat ruler which every so often he touches between my legs to make sure I keep them apart. He tells me that he wants a good view and to lift my bottom for him. As I do so, he pulls the knickers down a bit more and starts to smack me across the pussy which I really enjoy, so he continues until I have the most tremendous orgasm."

Leonard is almost speechless as he utters the usual finish line: "Right, right, now Angela, when I click my fingers you will sit up and you will not remember anything you have told me."

"How was I, Mr Laleham? Do you think you'll be able to help me?"

"Very good, Angela. I think that's probably enough for me today, I mean for you, today. Let's make another appointment

for next week and take it from there, ok?"

We were both laughing by this point and Miles said he couldn't wait for the next instalment. Then he fell asleep.

Day 8 – Monday 30th September
8.12 am
Back to the old routine! Miles has left for work and I am sipping tea pondering the slight drizzle that is misting the window, wondering if I will bother cycling today, or not.

Only two days to work. I wasn't lying when I told Miles that the students had a reading week. I'm supposed to be marking assignments and polishing up my lectures. The powers that be want more modern art on the syllabus, so I could find myself in the horrible position of debating the highs and lows of Laurent Fournier!

Ping! Email from Luce.

> *Hiya Bethy Baby*
>
> *Have booked your flight. Details attached. We're going to have fun, I promise! (Yeh sure Luce, sorting out Laurent)… and I simply must introduce you to Jerry, darling! (Who?) … My therapist says I should write things down, Rob swears by it, says it helps put things into perspective, so I have sent you one about Jerry – hope you like it, but hands off haha!*
> *Luv Luce xxxx*

Oh no! She's writing stories too. I can just imagine their content. Lunchtime reading I think! Still, it's really kind of her to organise the flight. Okay, off to work.

Lunch

Place is dead. Most of the staff have taken the week off. Bliss. Peace and quiet. Julie is off too, thank goodness, or she would have wanted to trade stories about the weekend. That's a win!

Someone has stuck up a poster about Laurent's exhibition. The dates for London are 7–13 October. A week today. Edinburgh 13–19 January. I feel like ripping it off the wall, but then I'd have to explain. Most people here don't know about our connection. Julie does, so it can't have been her. Damn. At least the poster has a tasteful scene from the garden at Uzes, thank goodness. It was a lovely garden and the cottage … Enough, enough!

Luce's story …! Like Rob, she writes in third person, maybe gives her a sense of distance. More likely, it could all be fiction, total fantasy on her part. She does describe the house very well. Beautiful and definitely not child friendly.

11. *"Lucinda at the Market"*

Lucinda was at the market early, knowing that otherwise the plumpest cherries, the sweetest strawberries, and the delicious new Victoria plums, would all have been sold. The late summer sun was already warm on her face but there was just a hint of approaching autumn in the bright bunches of dahlias and pots of chrysanthemums beside the fruit stall. Jerry treated her to one of the special smiles he saved for his regular, female, customers. "Good to see you, darlin' – what can I do for you this lovely morning'?" he winked exaggeratedly, "in the fruit and veg line, o' course!"
Lucinda laughed with him at the familiar joke. Jerry was popular in the town, especially among the women, he knew they liked to be chatted up a bit, especially the not-quite-so-young ones, so he did his best to make them smile. It didn't do sales any harm, either.

Tanned from being outside all year round, muscular from hefting heavy boxes all day, Jerry was of medium height which was another point in his favour as far as Lucinda was concerned, she liked to look a man in the eye, more or less, to feel his erection hard against her stomach when they embraced.

Jerry was looking particularly tasty this morning, Lucinda thought, wondering what it would be like to tangle her fingers through his brown curls. Jerry snapped open a paper bag, jolting her out of her reverie.

"What's it to be?" he asked, and she came out in goosebumps under the scrutiny of his blue, blue eyes. Having chosen what she needed for the weekend, Lucinda browsed the stall while Jerry weighed and bagged her choices. Pausing in front of a box of long cucumbers Lucinda picked up the straightest and ran one hand up and down its length several times, while circling its base with the thumb and forefinger of her other hand.

"Hard enough for you?" Looking up she saw Jerry smiling at her.

"Absolutely," she replied coolly, handing the cucumber to him and he tucked it into the box he was packing with her purchases. "Anything else?"

"Not for now," Lucinda told him, a little wistfully. Jerry picked up two large and very ripe figs and weighed them slowly in the palm of his hand, his eyes on her face.

"Present for a good customer," he grinned and placed them on the top of the box. "You'll find they're delicious, and soft as silk, suck them gently…" Their eyes locked, and Jerry asked, "Is that your car in front of the pub? I'll carry this lot over for you."

As he stowed the box into the car boot Jerry pressed his business card into Lucinda's hand, leaving his own hand in hers a moment longer than necessary.

"I do home deliveries for special customers," he told her, and with another wink turned back to the queue at his stall.

Lucinda thought about Jerry all the way home, deciding that she might just ask for a home delivery next time, and remembering the cucumber she giggled, squirming on her seat. At red traffic lights she pushed an exploratory finger high between her thighs, feeling how moist her lips there were.

"Better change these wet knickers when I get in," she thought, "might be a good idea to give that cucumber a satisfaction test, too …"

The cucumber test had been a success. Lucinda hadn't put it away in the larder with the other shopping but left it on the kitchen table while she put the kettle on. Between sips of coffee she regarded the cucumber thoughtfully for a few minutes and then, draining her cup, got up to riffle through a drawer. Finding the chopping board, a sharp knife and the vegetable peeler she lay the cucumber on the board and stroked its smooth skin. It was about fifteen inches long, thick and weighty.

Lucinda twisted off the little remnant of stalk at one end and began peeling it, with long firm strokes, to about half its length, leaving a good eight inches to hold. Making sure the front and back doors were locked, Lucinda carried the cucumber into the bedroom and laid it on a towel on the bedside table. After closing the shutters she made a nest of pillows against the headboard and folded back the duvet, then quickly slipped off her pink ballet slippers and wriggled out of the pale blue leggings. Settling herself against the pillows Lucinda glanced up at the large mirrored doors of the wardrobes, and smiled at her reflection.

Drawing up her legs she let her knees fall open, revealing her glossy pussy, the lips parting slightly, hinting at the hidden folds. The glistening shaved cucumber slid inside her easily, cool and firm.

"Cucumber is great for the skin," she thought, "I call this a special beauty treatment …" It made a change from her

pink Rampant Rabbit – although the ears on the rabbit were an inspired addition. Reaching for her expectant clit Lucinda expertly brought herself to a climax and lay looking in the big mirrors at the cucumber still between her thighs.

"Mmm, now there's a small problem, I can't use that item in the salad tonight. But I know where I might get another …"

Jumping up she found Jerry's business card in her bag and quickly dialled his number. The noises of the market were still audible and Lucinda smiled into the 'phone.

"Jerry? So glad I caught you – this is Lucinda Dale, you gave me your card earlier… oh good, you remember! Jerry, I need another cucumber – yes – and a head of celery, celery goes so well with Brie, don't you think? You know, that slightly salty, creamy taste of very ripe Brie on the tongue? Half an hour? Fab, see you then," and she rattled off her address.

Lucinda flew around the bedroom, smoothing the bed linen and plumping the pillows; cracking open the shutters a little to afford privacy but allow just enough of the morning sun to filter though. After a quick shower, soaping her body with Rose by Roger and Gallet, Lucinda stepped into the bedroom and sprayed a mist of the same scent into the air before walking through it, so that the tiny beads of attar of roses settled on her hair and body. The elusive light fragrance was just right for daytime, Lucinda considered. Quickly dressing in lacy French knickers and matching bra in a soft nude colour, which blended with her skin, she slid a cream linen shift dress over her head and stood back to admire the result. The linen was slightly opaque, the outline of her body just discernible, seeming as if she was naked beneath it. Brushing out her thick chestnut bob, a slick of lip gloss and mascara were all that was needed to accentuate her light tan, and she was ready. Slipping her feet into simple pewter leather sandals, she ran downstairs just as the doorbell rang. Jerry stood on the step, a paper carrier in his arms.

"Home delivery for Lucinda Dale," he grinned as Lucinda opened the door.

"Wonderful! Come in …" Lucinda held open the door as Jerry followed her inside, "would you bring them to the kitchen for me?"

"Very nice – very smart," Jerry looked around him apprecia-tively at the old elm floors and carefully restored period features mixed with furnishings of leather and linen and antique wood. The colour palette throughout the old town house was of toning neutrals, with a vibrant splash of colour in each room – lime green cushions on a sofa, cobalt blue glass on an old limed-oak dresser, a big bowl of fragrant late roses in pinks and yellows on the kitchen table. The air smelled deliciously of wax polish and flowers, and wood ash from the log fire the evening before.

"Thanks." Lucinda smiled, "but the Georgians usually got it right, didn't they? Proportions, and all that?"

"They did," Jerry agreed, putting the bags on the kitchen table next to the roses, his eyes on Lucinda's own proportions, "sorry if the cucumber you bought earlier wasn't good enough."

"Oh, it was!" Lucinda assured him, "I just can't use it in the salad to go with supper tonight, now. What do I owe you?"

"We'll settle up later," Jerry said, then, "I really like these old places. And the way you've done this one up."

"Interiors are my thing, really. Would you like to look round, have you time?" Lucinda asked, thinking, 'this is easy, like a game of tennis, returning the shots to each other, moving the game along…'

"Love to, and I do. My brothers and the other lads are looking after the stall. I can leave them to it for once."

Lucinda led Jerry back to the hall, up the curving staircase and into her bedroom on the first landing. Jerry took in the big French bed, with white lines and a faux fur throw folded across the foot of it; a tall four-stemmed white orchid, in a glass

66

bowl on top of a chest of drawers, reflected in the big mirror behind it; the wall of mirrored doors, and the chandelier of Murano glass casting a kaleidoscope of colours across the ceiling.

"Wow," he said simply, turning to Lucinda beside him.

"You've dust on your cheek," she said, reaching up to brush it off. Jerry turned his head and kissed her fingers, holding her wrist firmly.

"Glad you rang – nice surprise when I wasn't expecting it."

"You must be hot after being in that sun all morning – let's take this off," and Lucinda started to unbutton his shirt, but Jerry pulled back a little.

"I probably need a shower."

"You smell good to me," Lucinda pulled him back close to her and carried on unbuttoning, "sort of citrussy, nice. You can have a shower later!"

Jerry held her face in his hands and kissed her, gently at first and then harder as her fingers fumbled at his belt. Slipping out of his shirt, and kicking off his shoes, Jerry stood in bare feet on the thick cream carpet as Lucinda loosened his belt and undid his jeans. His erection was straining to escape his fly and Lucinda tucked her hands inside his pants to cup his buttocks. Jerry's gasp encouraged her and with a deft movement she slid his pants and jeans down his legs. He stepped out of them and stood gloriously naked in front of her.

Bending, Jerry lifted the hem of her dress in both hands, drawing it slowly up over her body, admiring her soft curves as they were revealed. Having draped the dress over a chair he unhooked her bra and released her breasts, kissing each in turn.

"Just lovely," he murmured, nuzzling her neck, and kissed her again, his tongue parting her lips. In a swift movement he picked her up and carried her to the bed, climbing on to it beside her.

"I'm slightly surprised you didn't just bend me over the kitchen table, or take me on the stairs," Lucinda whispered, close to his ear.

"The first time should be comfortable, and in bed," Jerry told her, spreading her legs and kneeling between them, bending his head to her wet pussy, licking in practised sweeps of his tongue from her ass to her clit. Lucinda almost forgot to breathe as he rested his head on the inside of one thigh, his soft brown curls like silk against her skin. With one hand he gently opened her folds, and then bent to kiss her lips there as though they were her mouth. His tongue probed inside her before his mouth fastened on her clit as a baby might onto a nipple, and sucked hard, his tongue drawing her willing little twist of sensitive flesh and nerves up into his mouth.

Lucinda's hands were in his hair, her body jerking in spasms of pure delight as Jerry moved forward and whispered, "Now, taste yourself," before pressing his wet mouth on hers, their tongues colliding. His hard cock brushed her thigh and she reached down to stroke its length. With her other hand she gently rubbed his cock against her clit and then pushed it down, thrusting her buttocks up to take him inside her.

Jerry sank into her with a groan as Lucinda demanded, "Fuck me hard, Jerry! Fuck me as hard as you can…"

OMG Luce! I don't think I'll be able to eat cucumber ever again!

Think I'll tidy up here and head off home soon.

6.39 pm
It was drizzling rain when I left college but had a lovely walk back home. Went via a few charity shops. Saw Muriel in the hospice bookshop – she had set aside a volume of poetry by Wallace Stevens that she thought I would like. So kind. I was hoping to buy some of her home-made Scottish tablet to give to Luce but there was none left. She gave me the recipe, so I popped into Waitrose to get some condensed milk, vanilla and granulated sugar. Bought a few other goodies bedsides, but no cucumbers!

Miles came home and caught me in the kitchen.

"Great smell Beth. What you making?"

"Well, there's a Waitrose Salmon en Croute in the oven for dinner but I'm making tablet!"

"Why?"

"For Luce."

"Oh, what about the twins?"

"What about them?"

"Did you get something for them too?"

I turned back to stirring the sugar, avoiding his eyes.

"Oh you know Miles, they get so much. Luce buys them all the latest gadgets and stuff. It's hard to know what to get. I'll wait 'til I see them and take it from there," I lied. I was so glad that he couldn't see my face.

He came up behind me, put his arm round my waist and nuzzled into the back of my neck.

"I'm going to miss you so much. What I wouldn't give to fuck you on the kitchen table right now!"

"I would love that too, Miles, but I need to keep stirring for another twenty minutes!"

"Remember the melted chocolate?" How could I forget?

"I think you need a cold shower Miles!"

He tossed his head back and laughed.

"Okay I know when I'm not wanted. I'm going to watch the news!" With that, he slapped me on the bum and left me to my stirring,

I spent the next twenty minutes daydreaming about kitchen sex.

Day 9 – Tuesday 1st October
12.37 am

Very tired. Finished making the tablet. Miles licked the pan and ruined his appetite for dinner! Cuddled up on the sofa and watched Game of Thrones. Miles has a thing for Cersei Lannister. Says he likes strong women. I reminded him that she sleeps with her brother! We slumped off to bed around eleven and I recounted my memories of the chocolate episode.

12 *"Chocolate"*

The afternoon sun was fading and I was singing to myself in the semi gloom, enjoying the fun of stirring and melting the chocolate on the stove, eating as much as I was making. You came home early with a bunch of red roses, as you often did back then, you sneaked up behind me, gathered me round the waist and kissed my neck. I could smell the faint musk of your aftershave and a deep tingling unfurled in my belly. I stuck a finger in the chocolate and scooped some into your mouth. You licked it off greedily and sucked my finger longingly.
"I know a fellow who would love a taste of this," you said.
"And I know a lady who would like some too," I answered.
You slowly unbuttoned my shirt and I could feel you stirring. I took off your trousers and with a lot of mess and a lot of giggles, I coated your swelling cock with warm melted chocolate and went down on my knees and licked you, slowly and gently, using my lips and tongue until you were all aquiver and spurted happily like a dolphin! Then it was my turn. You lifted me onto the kitchen table opened my legs and poured chocolate around my already wet pussy. It was an ecstasy of warmth and juiciness and you licked me slowly at first, then firmly and more firmly. Round you went with your lips and tongue and I cried in delight until you were ready again and we came together like pounding waves on a moonlit beach and all was

calm and peaceful again, the dark of the evening settling around our tired bodies. And you carried me upstairs and ran a hot bath, soapy and sweet and smelling of jasmine and, like little sand boys messed from play, we bathed and washed the chocolate from our hair and lay down on the bed all cosy and warm and slept until we were ready to play again.

"I'm ready to play," he said, and then he made beautiful love to me.

I am lying here, in the wee small hours, writing and hoping. I don't want to lose this.

Day 9 – Tuesday 1st October
8. 12 am
Usual start to the day. Miles has left and I am drinking tea in bed.

Ping! Email from Miles.

"My Beth"

Last night was perfect and you were exquisite. As you stood there naked before me I was taken aback by how beautiful you are. More beautiful than when we were married, even. Then we embraced and kissed. Your bottom felt so soft and smooth. You lay on the bed and I gazed at your body in wonder. I moved my eyes down. The dark, wispy hair against your pale skin – just beautiful. You parted your legs slightly and looked so inviting, I was fully ready to pay homage.
It was magical when we made love. It's magical that you satisfy all my senses – all five.
Sight – not just your gorgeous body, but your beautiful face.
Hearing – the little moans you breathe as we make love and when I hear you say you adore me, tears of joy well up.

*Taste – the taste of your lips and of course when I put my
tongue inside you and you taste like good wine.*
*Smell – the smell of your musky perfume and the lovely rich
smell of your juices.*
*Touch – of course the fleshy feel of you against me, but also
the light touch of your hand on my chest or when you fondle
my side and make me spasm.*
*And when I climaxed inside you last night it felt as strong as
I've ever known. It seemed to go on and on. Forcing myself
deep into you.*
*And lying next to you, laughing and making plans, I felt so in
love with you. And then we made love again. From behind,
fast, urgent but very satisfying.*
    M xxxxxxxx

I feel like weeping. How can I answer this when I've been so
deceitful?

My Darling Miles

*The tenderness of your email is making me cry. Last night was
wonderful for me too, my love.*
    Your Beth xxxxx

I can't face going into work. I need to talk to somebody. I feel
like I'm cracking up.

I'm going to 'phone Imo later and see if I can meet up with her.
I'll make some toast, go back to bed and read the book of poems
I bought yesterday. Must thank Muriel and tell her the tablet
recipe was a success.

11.37 am
Heading over to Imo's for coffee. Will cycle – it's a lovely day,

72

need to blow away the cobwebs. Have a line of poetry stuck in my head… 'Out of this same light, out of the central mind, We make a dwelling in the evening air, In which being there together is enough.' Miles and me, being there together is enough.

5.49 pm
I'm back home.

Imo was so pleased to see me. She had baked some scones and made a huge cafetière of coffee. Her lounge is so comfy, you just sink into the sofas and there was a log fire burning even though it wasn't that cold. I was tired from the cycle up the hill and grateful for a seat.

"Well Beth, what's up?" She knew me well enough to know there was something wrong.

"Laurent."

"What about Laurent?"

"I don't want him to show the paintings."

"That's why you're going to London?"

I nodded.

"Would it be so bad if he did?"

"Miles! I couldn't hurt him like that."

"He's a grown man Beth, I'm sure he would understand."

"But you don't see. I told him that the paintings were destroyed. He would be so upset to find out that I lied to him."

"He would understand. He loves you. He knows how painful that episode was for you and how you wanted to erase things from your mind."

She was right, of course.

"I don't want them on display. I couldn't bear it."

"So really, it's about you Beth, not about Miles?"

"You can be so hurtful Imo! Why is it about me?"

"Be honest with yourself Beth," she patted my hand … "you know I will never give you an easy answer, that's why you've come to see me." Right again … "Why are you really going to London? Are you curious to see the portraits again after so many years, are you curious to see Laurent?"

"What do you mean?"

She leaned back into the sofa and sipped her coffee.

"The last time you came to see me you were bored. Your sex life was dull and practically non- existent. You wanted Miles to desire you; you were dreaming of changing his mind about having babies. Think about it. Here comes Laurent, dredging up all those memories of Paris, of Uzes … of your pregnancy. It doesn't take a psychologist to see the attraction for you."

"That's not fair Imo. I love Miles. Laurent was a bastard!" Yet something in what she said hit me very deep.

"You didn't feel like that back then, Beth. You were besotted. He was a great lover, adventurous, daring, exciting, you said so yourself. You had never met anyone like him, and Laurent loved you as much as he could ever love anyone. We were all amazed when he actually married you Beth, his infidelity was in his genes, for goodness sake."

It had surprised me too.

"And as for the baby, Laurent was totally bereft. I don't think he ever got over it. He hid those portraits for years. He couldn't bear to look at your pregnant belly and the love in your eyes. He poured himself into those paintings and if he feels strong enough to show them now, then you should be too."

"Why do you defend him Imo?"

"I'm telling you the truth. I was with you in those awful months after you left. You could barely see a way of living, without the baby and without Laurent. It took months for Luce and I to get you back to health. By then of course, Laurent had descended into a drunken mess. Be very careful before you open the door to the past Beth."

I scoffed. "Ha! You think I could be tempted?"

Imo said nothing.
"I've lied to Miles about my reason for going."

Imo stayed silent.
"I told him I was going to see the twins."
"Lies just beget lies, Beth." She echoed my own thoughts. " You don't have to go. You could just tell Miles the truth."
It was my turn to stay silent.
"Well, I'm sure you'll do the right thing." She turned the conversation around. "Would you like more coffee and tell me, how are the stories going?"

5.49 pm
When I left Imo's, there were so many thoughts racing through my head. I've decided to go ahead with the trip. Even if she's right in what she said, I need to get rid of my demons. Maybe seeing Laurent and the paintings again will help me draw a line under everything; I was looking forward to a few days of luxury with Luce.

After Imo's, I cycled across to the New Town, bathed in the soft autumnal light that coats the sandstone with a creamy pink hue. I stopped at Muriel's charity shop and found her sitting alone behind the counter reading *Lady Chatterley's Lover*! Strange choice I thought, but I was soon to be enlightened!

"Hello Beth. We're very quiet today. I was just about to have a cuppa. Would you like one?"

I was still waterlogged from Imo's but didn't want to disappoint.
"That's great, thank you."

"There's a little kitchen at the back. Come on through, we'll easily hear if someone comes in." The door has an old fashioned bell. "I've got some of that instant chocolate you see on the adverts."

She held up a box.

"That would be lovely." I was getting used to lying.

"So how was the book?"

"Perfect, Muriel. It's so good of you to find these things for me!"

"Happy to help! And how did the tablet go?"

"Lovely! Did as you said, kept stirring until it got thick. Miles ate so much of it, he went right off his dinner!"

"Nothing would put my Cedric off his dinner... except maybe... Well never mind, here's your drink. Would you like some whippy cream on the top?"

"Em ... no thanks."

"I'm going to be naughty and have some." She piped a large swirl of cream into her cup.

I smiled as Muriel sipped her hot chocolate.

"What is it, dear?" asked Muriel.

"Cream moustache."

"Oh, thank you," Muriel wiped away the cream with a napkin.

"So what did Cedric get you for your birthday?" I remembered from our last conversation.

"Pearl earrings. Like them?" Muriel turned her head and pulled back her platinum bob a little to show me the earrings.

"Very nice."

"I asked him for a pearl necklace."

"Oh. Well maybe next birthday. Or Christmas."

"No dear. A *pearl necklace*," repeated Muriel, putting heavy emphasis on each word.

"When you say pearl necklace, you don't mean ...?" I lowered my voice.

"That's exactly what I mean, dear," said Muriel crisply.

"Muriel!" I feigned shock.

"What? We're still … er … active, you know?"

"I'm glad."

"Oh yes. Every fortnight. Friday. After Newsnight," Muriel was talking to herself now as much as to me, "Lights off. Pyjama bottoms down. Ten minutes. Then straight to sleep. Very brisk and efficient. Very Cedric."

"Well, that sounds very nice."

"Yes. Very nice. We've been married for over forty years. I wanted to try something a bit more adventurous."

"Okay."

"So," Muriel lowered her voice and leaned forward a little, "a couple of weeks ago we went to a party. A swingers party. A masked swingers party."

"Really? What happened?"

"Well, we got there. We were expecting a mansion or something like that. It was a semi a few miles out of town."

"And? What happened when you got there?"

"There were quite a few people. Couples mainly. Dressed in everyday clothes, wearing little black masks. Like the Lone Ranger."

"But what happened?"

"Cedric chose first. Blonde woman around forty. Slim. He took her upstairs and came down ten minutes later. Knowing him it was all very brisk and efficient."

"And?"

"Well I liked the look of the man next to me. He was young and had long hair and stubble. He took me upstairs."

"How old was he?"

"Twenty five maybe. We were up there for an hour. Three times he had me. He said I was much more fun than girls his own age. He said I knew things. He was lovely. Big boy too."

"I don't know what to say."

"Don't say anything, Beth. I told Cedric I think we should go again."

77

"What did he say?"

"He said he'd better pay a visit to your lovely husband. Get a prescription for some little blue tablets."

"Does he need them?"

"Well actually," Muriel smiled, "on Monday he suggested an early night. He took me upstairs and made love to me so passionately it was like we'd turned the clock back thirty years. He missed Newsnight."

I could hardly keep a straight face. It was a welcome relief from the seriousness of my visit to Imo. Helped to lighten my mood as I cycled home. I'm still smiling as I write this. Must tell Miles later! Time to make dinner. Something easy? Spag Bol ... maybe I should give up being a veggie for the next few days.

Day 10 – Wednesday 2nd October
12.53 am
Miles is asleep. I am sitting up in bed, wide awake. Despite the fact I'm going away tomorrow he seemed quite upbeat. I think he feels more confident about the inquiry on Friday. He says most of the attention will be on Bill and Shonagh.

He tucked into the Spag Bol and was pleased there was enough left over for tomorrow so he wouldn't have to cook!

What happened tonight? It was a good evening really. After dinner (no alcohol!) Miles made cappuccino (decaf!) using the Pavoni. We sat on the sofa feeling very smug at our restraint. The flight is at 9.45 and Miles offered to take me to the airport before going to work. I wanted to take the bus or even a taxi but he insisted. We decided we would have an early night. We watched a bit of the news ... Scottish girl in court in Peru for drug smuggling ... Miliband still going on about his father ... Princess Diana kept a sex diary about the royal family... Now that *was* interesting.

78

"You're in good company Beth."

"Indeed I am! Talking of sex, I went to see Muriel at the charity shop today and she was reading *Lady Chatterley's Lover*." I didn't tell him about Imo.

"Hmmm"

"Does that not surprise you Miles?"

"Nothing surprises me. I'm a doctor, remember?"

I punched him playfully in the stomach, yet it echoed Imo's words.

"She and Cedric go to swingers' parties."

"Hmmm."

"She said Cedric was going to see you about getting some little blue pills. Do you think we'll still be up for it when we're their age Miles?"

"Don't see why not! Could be interesting if they manage to sort out the female Viagra, we could be at it into our nineties!"

"Oh God, doesn't bear thinking about."

Miles burst out laughing. "I'm just thinking about Muriel and Cedric at their swingers' parties."

"What do you think they get up to?"

"No idea!"

"Do you fancy going to one?"

"Definitely not – I might end up with Muriel!"

I think I'll make up some stories about M&C, to give Miles a laugh.

Bedtime was subdued. I asked Miles if he would like a story. He asked for one with Cersei Lannister … I said he should be so lucky, but I looked through Imo's selection and there was one that seemed quasi Game of Thrones. He said that would do. So I read:

13. "*The Homefires*"

… Jungen's heart raced as he approached the citadel of Tharn. The road was desolate and fire had scorched the earth. What

would he find? Would the standard be flying? And what about Lilas? He dared not think.

Slowly they trudged onward, Morg's halting breath clouded the air but still he pulled his master on.

Finally, they reached the brow of the hill, the sun setting into blood red rivers across the molten sky, and there she stood in all her granite glory, his home, his haven, imperious as ever, a golden standard waving from the spire that lanced the heavens. It was safe.

A renewed energy raced through his veins and together they ran the final hurdle. A mangy hound came to meet them, lapping at their heels.

"What? Is it you, Fliver, my old friend?" He ruffled the dog's matted hair and gripped him close.

They walked through the battered gates, a faint smell of smoke hung about the air. A lone brazier burned dimly in the hall.

"Is anybody there?" His words echoed around the barren hallway.

Jungen held his breath. He could not hope.

A soft rustling came from behind.

"Is it truly you, my Lord?"

His absence had not been easy for her. The bloom of her cheek had gone and her silver hair shone blankly in the gloom. Her clothes were torn but clung to her body in fierce defiance.

He turned, and when she saw his face she fell to her knees and wept.

"Lilas, my love. I am home."

She ordered the old servant to boil some water and they filled the tub with herbs and oils to soothe his battered bones.

Lilas took his sword, loosening his belt until the heavy cloak fell to the ground. His garments were hardened and thick with blood but slowly she teased them from his skin, kissing each wound with soft, red lips. Naked, he climbed into the soothing water and she washed him clean. He had once dreamt of heaven but this was paradise indeed.

She wrapped him in a cloak of Mordelle hair and led him into the chamber. There she fed him on the little food she had, some meal and a few old figs. He bit into the flesh, still sour and fetid but they tasted like manna to his starved soul. Lilas kissed the juice from his lips. She smelled of musk and candle wax. A fire burned in the huge fireplace, sticks from the old table, broken in honour of his return. No other light shone in the heavy room. He took the cloak from his shoulder and placed it on the floor. The heat from the fire warmed his broken skin. Lilas unfastened her braid. The long tendrils of hair danced in the firelight and fingered her soft white shoulders. Only a few clasps held her robes in place and Lilas pulled them free, allowing them to fall to the ground. Her young, thin body stood before him, a marble statue in perfection. Small breasts, with pale, pink nipples, cold and forgotten. Her smooth belly, flawless and pure, leading to the mound of silver hair that beckoned him close.

He kissed her softly, bringing warmth to her soul and colour to her cheeks. He sucked her cold nipples and they turned red and hard. She began to feel warm for the first time in many a long day. The wetness between her legs felt like a thousand wild dreams to Jungen and he laid her down and entered her. And if there were no future and no past, only the here and now, he would gladly die. And they lay together and came together, again and again until the fire died. He wrapped the cloak around them and they clasped each other tight, tight, and would never let go, never again.

"I'm going to miss you, wife," said Miles.

"I'll miss you too, husband," I replied.

He gathered me in his arms and fell asleep.

I've been lying awake for ages, just watching him. And thinking. I'm going to sleep now. I have downloaded *Lady Chatterley's Lover* to my Kindle (free!) … read it years ago as a teenager, but will read it again on the plane. Just as well no-one can tell what you're reading and if it's good enough for Muriel…

10. 23 am
I'm on the plane. Delayed 30 mins. Have ordered a lovely breakfast. I'm used to having just a bottle of water and a sandwich in the economy seats, but I could've had three G&Ts by now if I'd wanted, or needed! A very smart lady in a business suit has been knocking them back since take off. Maybe she has a fear of flying … haha … just remembered … Erica Jong and the zipless fuck! Should download that one as well, to get some ideas!

So far, the whole storytelling plan has gone very well. Miles thought it was stupid at first, but he has warmed to the idea – he now expects his bedtime story every night! Mustn't disappoint while I am away. He was so sweet this morning, brought me tea early, drove out to the airport and came all the way with me to departures. He looked so forlorn as I hugged him goodbye. Told him it was just 'til Saturday and he said he'd come and pick me up, even though he'll miss the football! He is definitely more attentive! I'm going to read my Kindle now and enjoy all this amazing free food! Trying not to think of the problems ahead, enjoying the moment, as Luce would say.

11.35 am
Almost time to land. Managed to read 50 pages of Lady C. Can't see what all the fuss was about. Imo's airplane story is much more raunchy! I wonder if this is what's meant as a zipless fuck …

14. *"Eight Miles High"*

Something very exciting happened to me last month on the flight back from Montreal. I had been speaking at a conference on digital imaging and was making my way back home to London. The flight was long and boring. I was watching Meg Ryan in 'French Kiss' on the TV screen and feeling a wonderful hard-on emerging.

The seat next to me was occupied by a sleeping female, all covered up in a blue fleecy blanket and a black blindfold over her eyes. Just as I was about to reach the point where I needed to hot foot it to the toilet to jerk off, she grabbed my hand and pulled it under the blanket. I felt the warmth of her naked belly, smooth and soft and she pulled my hand further down to the cosy depths of her moist fanny. It was not a landing strip but a full on hairy bush. She pushed my fingers inside her, it was soaking wet and pulsing so much I wished I could ram my cock in hard.

She guided my fingers to her clitoris and made me rub it round and round until I could feel it hard as bone. I thought I would burst out of my jeans. She moaned softly and pushed my fingers back and forth until I felt the tension break, then she grabbed my hand fiercely, digging her nails into my palm until my eyes watered. Then she released me, pushed my hand out, pulled the blanket tight, turned her back and went back to sleep. It was unbelievable.

I stood up, rather uncomfortably as my hard-on was pretty full, and made it to the toilet. I could taste her on my fingers as I jerked off over the sink, mixing my spunk with her juice. I washed up, got back to my seat and watched the end of the movie.

Must ask Luce if this has ever happened to her!

3.10 pm

I am sitting in the Palm Court tearoom at the Ritz, waiting for Lucinda. She sent Jules to pick me up at the airport because she was running late. He was to collect me and bring me here. I've always wanted to see my name on a piece of card held up at the arrivals gate, and got such a surprise to see in big red letters, BETH RODGERS, held by a six foot two hunk in a chauffeur's uniform! What a welcome. Traffic was slow due to roadworks and a traffic jam. The drive took almost two hours. There was a bottle of champagne and two glasses. Jules insisted that I have a drink while he drove. I kept seeing his gorgeous brown eyes in the mirror and just knew that Lucinda and he... Here she comes now, better put the diary away!

9.15pm
At Lucinda's. Have escaped to my bedroom for a bit of much needed quiet time before supper. Glad I took my laptop. Miles has been in touch. He's missing me! To be honest, I haven't had time to miss him, until now. Luce has put me in my 'old bedroom', the one I lived in for three months after Uzes. It's been decorated several times since then and brings back no memories, thankfully, except for the view over the park which has changed little. I need Miles, I need the comfort of his arms around me. He wants to Skype but if I see him, I'll burst into tears. He says he'll send me a bed-time story later!

I have eaten so much today and poor Miles is having the leftover Spag Bol. Tea at The Ritz was fabulous, a bit like being on a film set. Luce of course seems to live her life in front of that invisible camera and she was perfectly at home walking onto the stage, flinging her arms around me in a cloud of cashmere and Lancôme's 'Midnight Rose.'

"Oh, Babes! How simply lovely to see you?" she shouted. "How was the traffic? Sorry I had to send Jules." She then spent the next two hours talking non-stop in between eating and drinking. I'm sure the other guests were wildly entertained!

She's calling me down for drinks ... Arghh... not more champagne I hope!

Midnight.

Have had enough of Luce! Had hoped Rob would be here but he's not home 'til tomorrow. After hours of chatting and several glasses of fizz, she'd finally noticed I was tired.

"It's so lovely to see you Beth, but – I have to say this – you do look the teensiest bit tired. Still gorgeous, of course, but not your usual self. And you're very quiet – Worrying about Laurent?"

"Of course."

"It'll be fine Beth. Rob's arranged dinner tomorrow night, a foursome, so you'll be quite safe!"

It is a shock, the thought of actually seeing him again. She asked after Miles,

"How's that well-endowed husband of yours?"

She would love a threesome, but never, never, never! I had to ask about the twins. And their school.

"They absolutely adore it, and then they adore me and Rob when they come home. In fact, we all adore each other, then, when the novelty wears a bit thin, it's time for a new term, and with luck another long haul trip for Rob ... then I can see Jerry ... and ... perfect!"

Luce loves to show off but I don't believe she's as bad as she'd like us all to think. We got on to the subject of therapists and I wish we hadn't. Too much information.

"... We have tried you know ... did I tell you Rob and I went to see a sex therapist, in Knightsbridge beautifully appointed, very plush décor, a la francaise ... you know the idea ... painting of a reclining nude above a white rococo fireplace and a love seat, upholstered in pink toile de jouy! ... more like a high class brothel and she the Madame, in her black and white Chanel suit and pearl necklace ... Rob couldn't take his eyes off her legs, said he had a hard-on the whole time … Anyway, we told her our problems, how we had to have sex at least twice a day, our threesomes with Tanya, Rob's airline sex, my obsession with Jerry … She offered us tea in china cups, asked a few questions and then said we'd come to the wrong therapist … she helped couples re-ignite lost desires … said we had no problem in that department and handed me a card for Sex Addicts Anonymous …"

Miles would find that funny and no doubt he would agree. Am I turning into a sex addict, with my stories, expecting Miles to perform? No, we could never be like Luce and Rob. We could never share … being there together is enough.

Miles' email:

> *Darling Beth*
> *Here is a story for you, my Sheherazade! Like the very first one you read to me. I know I fell asleep but I heard every word!*
> *Sleep well my love*
>   *Miles xxxxxx*
> *#Attached Aladdin doc.*

> *Dearest Miles*
> *I will read it with joy. Thank you!*
> *Here is one for you, Lord Chatterley … Enjoy!*
>   *Love Beth xxx*
> *#Attached Lord C doc.*

After I sent it, I realised that it's about a cuckolded husband who cannot satisfy his wife – not an inspired choice under the circumstances. I can be very stupid sometimes.

I'm going to read *Aladdin*.

15. "Aladdin"

Aladdin was a handsome young man of Persian blood. He had been watching a certain beautiful maid who sat sewing delicate lace in the bazaar for many weeks, each day hoping she may lift her gaze to his and their eyes meet in recognition of mutual desire. Today he thought he might try playing a haunting melody on the flute he carried everywhere with him; a song that wept of lost love and longing, a song to capture the heart of the fine-boned lacemaker. As the first notes carried through the covered market, she was not the only Arab girl to raise her head in wonder and, as Aladdin played on, she slowly rose and danced her way towards the mesmerising piper. He was captured beyond words as she swirled around him in an arousing spectacle of ancient musical interpretation. She seemed to move in time to the snakes rising from their charmers' baskets, they too entranced by the pipe's melodic pitch. In the time honoured fashion, almost hypnotically, Leilia had chosen her husband.

A fine wedding gift of a silver lamp was given to the pair and Aladdin was told that whenever he chose to polish the lamp, his Genie would appear from the cave of wonder. Leilia now wore a shining amethyst ring handed down to her from her grandmother who had whispered a tale of old which spoke of granting wishes should she ever be in physical need. Their first night together as man and wife drew ever nearer and the newlyweds prepared themselves in the traditional fashion, smoothing perfumed oils on their expectant, honey-toned bodies. She wore a gown of fine lace which clung to her well-endowed breasts and enhanced her womanly hips swaying erotically as she now approached the silk-draped bed. He lay waiting for her dressed in gaucho pants of smooth silk, his chest bare and his heart pounding fit to burst. Leilia parted the *drapes and he was speechless at her beauty as she lay next to him, reaching for his hand. Unsure now, Aladdin rubbed the smooth, silver lamp next to the bed with his other hand, praying for magical powers. In an instant his bride lifted her gown and he knew in one glance that here was the cave of wonder – all he needed now was for his Genie to appear – which of course, with very little persuasion, she did. Leilia frantically kissed the amethyst ring, for now she was desperately in need, and made a wish for her husband's evident protrusion to carry her to the skies; he climbed upon her and they became one in a rush of requited love.*

I'm crying. I wonder how Miles is feeling, after reading Lord C. Have I made a mistake?

16. *"Lord Chatterley's Lover"*

… Sir Clifford Chatterley wheeled himself to the window and looked out. He saw his wife stride across the lawn and disappear into the woods.

There was a knock at the door.

"Come in Mrs Oldham," said Sir Clifford.

"Good afternoon, Sir Clifford," said Mrs Oldham, "time for your bed bath."

"Very well."

He wheeled himself over to the bed and with some effort got out of the chair and lay face down. Mrs Oldham removed his trousers and white drawers and lifted his undershirt up to his shoulders. She took a sponge and a bowl of warm, soapy water and began to wash his pale, naked body.

"You know where my wife is now, Mrs Oldham?"

"She's gone out, Sir Clifford."

"Yes. To the woods. Do you know what she's doing?"

"I can guess, Sir Clifford."

"I'm sure you can," he said bitterly, "she's gone to meet her lover. The gamekeeper. That bastard, Mellors."

"Yes, Sir Clifford."

"What should I do, Mrs Oldham?"

"Well, Sir Clifford. What's good for the goose…"

"What do you mean?" She said nothing and carried on washing his naked backside.

After a few minutes he said "what happened to your husband, Mrs Oldham?"

"Killed in the war, Sir Clifford."

"Has there been anyone since?"

"No. I loved him. I do miss the touch of a man though."

He looked at Mrs Oldham. She was a handsome woman in her mid fifties.

"Can I ask you something, Sir Clifford. Your terrible injuries, can you still….you know…get it up?"

"I don't know. All I know is I can't feel a damned thing below the waist."

She turned him over and looked with admiration at his naked-ness. His member was flaccid, but still very impressive.

"Perhaps we should find out, Sir Clifford."

"Very well."

She stroked his penis gently, but there was no effect.

"Let's see if we can help John Thomas out, shall we, Sir Clifford?"

Without a further word she began to undress. First her skirt, then her blouse. Then she slid down her panties and stood before Sir Clifford naked except for her black brassiere. Even though she was many years older than him, he found her hard, taut body most attractive.

She climbed onto the bed and took his hand. She pushed it between her legs and rubbed his fingers against her wetness. She gasped with pleasure.

"That feels nice, Sir Clifford."

"You have a beautiful, er…"

"It's my cunny, Sir Clifford. And it feels lovely, the way you rub me like that."

Sir Clifford looked down and, amazed, saw his penis rise and become erect. Mrs Oldham smiled.

"There, Sir Clifford. That's grand. Now, shall we see how that feels inside me?"

"Very well."

She climbed on top and slid herself down the shaft of his smooth erection. She started to ride him. Slowly at first. Then she slid down her brassiere so that it was around her midriff. She took his hands and rubbed them against her breasts with a circular motion. Then she fucked him with greater and greater urgency. It would be hard and quick. Purely physical. They both knew that.

She felt an ache, deep inside her, rise then ease. It was the first time she had made love to a man for many years. She could feel her climax approaching and moaned with delight.

Sir Clifford came first though. He didn't feel it but knew it happened and Mrs Oldham did too. She carried on fucking him as he stayed erect long enough for orgasm to rush through her aching body.

She bent forward and rested her forehead against his.

"So," he said, "you're Lord Chatterley's lover, eh?"

"Nay, Sir. Lord Chatterley's fucker.

Well it's too late now, I've sent it. I just have to hope that he sees the funny side of it. I'm tired and I feel confused. Tomorrow will be a long day, waiting for the dinner with Laurent. I wish I had never come – why didn't I just tell Miles the truth and I could be at home in his arms, instead of here …

Day 11 – Thursday 3rd October
7.20 am

Had a terrible night – combination of too much alcohol and too much confusion in my head. Feel no better after standing under Luce's power shower for twenty minutes – must get myself together. If I'm going to face Laurent, at least I have to look the part and Rob will be home today too, so desperate measures called for.

11.30 am

Managed to sneak out of the house without disturbing Luce and, dressed in track suit and trainers, jogged my way to the park to join the brigade of daily keep-fit enthusiasts already hard at it in the early morning gloom. Had to slow to a brisk walk after ten minutes but gradually felt my brain clear and began to enjoy the feel of London again. Text from Miles – 'So this is the Lady Chatterley you spoke of Beth! Still laughing…' I had a smile on my face when I got back, Luce of course looked none the worse for all of yesterday's antics – just another ordinary day for her!

"Look at you, all rosy and glowing! Smoothie or coffee, or both?"

I downed the smoothie, grabbed a croissant and made a swift exit, saying I needed an hour to get changed and have a bath, if that was ok.

"Treat the place like home darling, I'm out this morning and Rob won't be home 'til after lunch – enjoy!"

Luce's place is like living in a hotel, so I made the most of it and, with a bit of effort, managed to transform my tired face and blow-dry my hair into an off-the-face style that suited my mood. I was determined that, when I met Laurent, I was going to appear a confident, woman of the world, far removed from the fragile creature of ten years before. One of my favourite boutiques was just round the corner so I'm heading off to choose a simple under-stated outfit for tonight, I'll worry about justifying it to Miles later!

6.45 pm
Spent the afternoon chatting with Rob. He was full of anecdotes and obviously felt he had to entertain me in Luce's absence – maybe he was trying to put me at ease about tonight's dinner:

"Laurent had us all falling about the last time we met up, Beth. He was telling us how the life drawing classes were always such a dreadful bore. You could look but you couldn't touch and if you couldn't touch then how the hell could you convey your feelings. He said it was a bit like asking a chef to prepare his signature dish without letting him taste the ingredients on the way and how they always dragged in and unveiled the ugliest girl on the block! One to ones though, he said, were quite a different kettle of fish. The best one he ever had was when the older husband of a younger wife commissioned him to paint her nude. She loved it, found it somehow therapeutic to arrive at his studio, get her clothes off and pose for him. He found it a bit more than therapeutic. He said he honestly felt guilty about cashing the cheque but it was what you call a win, win, win situation. He was delighted, she was bloody delighted and Laurent was fucking delirious. Excuse the language, Beth, but the story wouldn't be the same without it."

Rob could see by my reaction that he'd overstepped the mark – as if I wanted to hear about Laurent's 'other' nudes! Perhaps Luce hadn't told him about Laurent's exhibition, or perhaps he'd just had one glass too many.

Getting mentally and physically prepared for tonight.

Half-past Midnight
It was the voice – it was always the voice, after all. Laurent stood up as I entered the busy restaurant and as soon as he spoke my

name and smiled, it was like I was twenty years old again, just briefly. He looked older, of course, but his new creased-up face suited him perfectly, tanned skin like elastic that just went back into place as the smile left. There was a sadness about him I didn't recall as we embraced like old friends and, as the evening went on, I almost forgot the very reason I was there – the Portraits! I needn't have worried with Luce there to blurt out exactly what she thought. Laurent was surprised for a moment but quickly recovered and spoke directly to me:

"I thought you'd be pleased, Beth. The portraits were judged my best back then and, if I'm honest, I don't think I've painted anything close to bettering them since. I should have asked you first perhaps, or warned you at least, to give you time to explain to, to … I always forget his name … Miles!"

The meal passed in a daze. One course followed another. Champagne, wine, fluid talk about art, Paris, Uzes. Laurent chatted easily. The studio, the cottage, everything was still the same he said. His voice was intoxicating. As we left the restaurant, he took me to one side and asked if I wanted to see the portraits. They were in storage, in a lock up just a short walk from the restaurant. Rob and Lucinda were in a drunken, amorous state and eager to get home. I agreed to walk with him. I just couldn't resist seeing them again. I felt quite safe. He had been part of my life for over four years, my husband for two – albeit a long time ago.

When the lights went on and he pulled off the drapes, the two portraits stood facing me. They were better than I remembered.

"You managed to repair the damage then?"

"It would take more than a little paint stripper to stop me, Beth."

I saw my twenty-two year old face staring back at me. Dark glossy hair, enigmatic smile. Naked body glistening in chiaroscuro, legs apart, one hand on my left breast and the other cradling my

93

pregnant stomach. I had lost the baby at 23 weeks. A little girl I called Aimee, big enough to move inside me, for Laurent to feel. The other photo he called his Madonna, me naked, sprawled on a chair, legs wide and gaping in a very provocative pose, hair splayed across my shoulders and a baby at my breast. I started to cry. He put his arms around me and I could smell the familiar aftershave, still the same.

"I've never loved anyone as much as I loved you then, Beth." The love was in the paintings. That's why they were his best.

"I'll never sell them. Never. I just want the world to see them, because they are beautiful. Because you are beautiful."

Sitting here now, wishing I couldn't hear Luce and Rob down the hall, still clearly enjoying themselves, I hear his words and see the portraits in my head.

Can't sleep. Pull a book off the shelf, one of Lucinda's carefully organised books, and find a story with an uncanny resemblance to real life, about another enigmatic beauty, a nude portrait and a troubled artist …

17. *"La Gioconda"*

"Come back to bed, Paul."
Mimi sprawled across the covers, her breasts hanging heavily on the pillows, legs wide and her dark pubic hair glistening in the pale light that shone weakly though the torn curtains.
"Not now, my love. I have to get to work. She will be waiting."
"Work. Work." She pouted. "Will I see you tonight?"
"Perhaps." He leaned over, kissed her warm forehead and threw some money on the dresser.
The sun was barely breaking through the grey winter sky and he pulled his coat around him. The stool and paint-box clattered against his legs as he hurried towards the marketplace. She

came at the same time every day and there she was, tapping her feet impatiently.

Paul set up the easel and she took her place on the stool, as usual. He knew her face by heart. Every line, every muscle, the little scar above her lip, the dark heavy eyebrows, her soft ruby lips, waiting to be kissed. But not by him. He sighed. She looked at him and he felt a slight blush creep over his cold cheeks. He busied himself with the task in hand. The portrait finished, she stood up, took the drawing and handed him a few coins. A slight drizzle began to mist his glasses. She took a piece of paper from her glove and placed it in his hand. Follow me, it said. Paul was puzzled but had little time to think. She was already walking quickly across the square, the black silk dress swishing at her ankles, showing a hint of scarlet petticoat and leather boots. He gathered his things and ran after her, dropping some brushes on the way, but not daring to stop, lest he lost sight of her.

She darted into an alleyway, scarcely looking back and he had to run to catch up. He caught sight of her turning into Rue Parlaine and then he lost her. Turning and searching, he finally glimpsed the hem of her dress and he followed her into a dark stairway leading to a set of rooms, small and sparsely furnished with only a small table, a chair and a low couch covered in dark green brocade. A small fire burned in the grate. She beckoned him to come and close the door.

Slowly she began to undress. Her mourning clothes were dark and heavy and the buttons difficult but soon the dress was discarded on the floor. She lifted it up and placed it on the chair. He then watched her unfasten the scarlet bodice until her small, firm breasts were naked. She lowered her petticoats to reveal a soft downy mound of pubic hair, the cool white of her thighs draped in sheer silk stockings. She lay down on the couch and closed her eyes. She meant for him to draw her. Stroke by stroke he traced the charcoal across the paper, the curve of her throat, the shape and shadow of her breasts, the nipples large and dark, the swell of her belly, white and round and the glorious depths of her sex where she laid one hand, poised to touch and caress herself. He kept control, immersing himself in the drawing until the final touch was done. She looked at it closely, examining every detail. She nodded. Yes it would do.

She took his hands and kissed the fingers one by one, cold, thin and blackened with charcoal. She lowered them down towards her thighs and Paul gasped as he reached inside and felt the warmth and wet of her. Pulling down his breeches, he knelt across and pushed himself into her, deep and firm, thrusting slowly and gently until she groaned and clung to his shirt. Her eyes were wild and bright as diamonds. He felt a shudder, like fear as she screamed and drew him to a climax.

No words were spoken. She loosened herself from his grasp, stood up and walked towards the chair. Paul lay on the couch and watched as she dressed. The putting on of the clothes made him rise again. She took no notice, quietly composing herself and then she folded the drawing into her glove. She left the room, without a glance.

Paul lay for a little while and then he, too, left the silent walls behind.

He never saw her again. Each time he tried to find the alley, the set of rooms, he failed. But he had the perfect image in his head, the map of her, and he drew her once more. And the painting, in oils, was never for sale, no matter the price.

Day 12 – Friday 4th October
7.00 am
Must have slept after that because my mobile woke me – it was Miles. He was so upset; apparently he'd seen a stupid photo on Luce's Facebook page of Laurent with his arm round me in the restaurant. If I didn't know her better I'd say she had done it on

purpose. Even worse, Miles checked the school holidays and knows the twins are not here! When I said I could explain everything, he just hung up and now he won't take my calls. Have decided to get a flight home ASAP – I need to see Miles face-to-face and tell him everything.

11.35 am
In the first class lounge at Heathrow. Managed to get the flight changed. Should get in around two-thirty. The inquiry is at three, so with any luck I can surprise Miles at the courthouse. Eating shortbread and sipping a white wine spritzer. Feeling gutted. Things are such a mess. My head hurts. Can't be bothered writing.

1.25 pm
On the plane. Have taken two paracetamols. No appetite. Will try and sleep.

8.59 pm
At home. Feeling so unwell. Can't stop crying. Rushed across town to see Miles and arrived just in time to see him getting into a taxi with Shonagh. He hasn't come home. Maybe they've just gone for a drink. His phone is switched off.

Day 13 – Saturday 5th October
1.29 am
Have been waiting all night. He's still not home. Hasn't been in touch. Got another stupid email from Luce apologising for the photograph. It doesn't even merit a reply. I'm going to bed. Am quite drunk.

8.39 am
No sign of Miles. I've gone beyond being upset. I'm angry now. Didn't waste much time, did he? Shonagh, of all people.

My head's still pounding but I'm not going to lie down to this. First Laurent and now Miles. Seeing the portraits brought back many memories, and I'm not so easily hurt these days. Necessity gives you a tough skin.

I'm starving. Had so little to eat yesterday and of course, there's no milk. I'll go out on the bike, clear my head and get breakfast somewhere.

11.36 am
Having breakfast in Toni's café on Morningside Road. Gave myself a really hard cycle run. Feeling much better after a strong Americano and a croissant. Looking out at the busy street, wondering where Miles is. Had a few texts from Luce and Imo. Haven't replied.

11.34 am
Text from Miles!

> >>>Where the fuck are you? I'm at the fucking airport!!!
> Oh God!
> >>>I changed flights and came home yesterday. Where the fuck were you???
> >>>Are you at home now?
> >>>No.
> >>>Where are you?
> >>>In a café.
> >>>Which one?
> >>>Toni's. Morningside.
> >>>Ok stay there I'll be 20 mins

I'm waiting for him. I see him driving past. He's parking across the road. He's getting out of the car and walking towards me. He looks tired and dishevelled, as if he's been up all night.

11.39 pm

Well, Miles came into the café, ordered an espresso and sat down heavily on the chair next to me. Nothing was said. Neither of us knew where to start. I decided to get in first.

"Are you going to tell me where you were last night? And before you say anything, I saw you getting into a taxi with Shonagh."

"I don't have to justify myself, Beth. You went to London, lying about the twins no less, and had dinner with Laurent. Do you expect me to just accept that?"

"I'm sorry I lied. I had my reasons."

"Well I had my reasons for getting into a taxi with Shonagh." Touché.

We were getting nowhere, trading insults, getting angry. I decided just to tell him the truth.

"I went to London to try and stop Laurent showing the portraits from Uzes. He's holding an exhibition at White Cube next week and then it's coming to Edinburgh in January.

"I thought they'd been destroyed."

"I lied."

"And did you?"

"What?"

"Stop him?"

"No."

"Why did you lie?"

"About the paintings or about London?"

"Both."

I'd had time to think about this over the past few days.

"I lied about the paintings because they are private and very personal to me. They represent a very painful time in my life. They could also be very embarrassing for you and I wanted to protect you. I had to lie about London because I'd lied about the paintings. One lie needed another."

"You could've told me."

I sat and played with the crumbs on my plate.

"What about you? Where were you last night? I waited and waited. I needed you and you never came home." I started to cry.

He took my hand and I pulled it away.

"I'd seen the photo on Facebook and was so angry with you, I could hardly think straight. The inquiry went very badly. They more or less said we'd let him down, the baby. Bill and Shonagh were deemed to have acted unprofessionally. The boyfriend will be charged with murder, the mother with wilful neglect. The journalists were all over us. Shonagh was really upset and I offered to take her home. We both needed a drink, so we had a couple of bottles of wine and then more. I think we ordered a Chinese. It's all a bit of a blur. I didn't mean to stay the night but I woke up on the sofa. Nothing happened."

I looked up and saw his face. He was telling the truth. I knew by his eyes.

"I walked about for ages this morning, trying to think straight. Then I went to the airport and you didn't come off the plane … I don't want to lose you, Beth."

"You haven't lost me Miles, there're just things we need to talk about." After seeing the portraits my feelings were so strong. I wanted a baby. But this was not the time to tell him.

"I'm going to cycle home. I'll see you there."

I got up and left.

It started to rain and by the time I got home I was soaked. Miles had run a bath and lit some candles. He held me close and I clung to him. I let him undress me and I stepped into the scented water. It was so warm and soothing I lay back and closed my eyes.

He sat on the edge of the bath and read to me. Something he wrote on our wedding day.

18. *"My Kind of Love"*

There's a kind of love that creeps upon you, like a whisper in the darkness and seeps under your skin to become a part of you that has always been there. And there's a kind of love that hits you, Bam! between the eyes, knocks you off your feet and takes your breath away. But the kind of love I have for you is all of this, and more, Those laughing eyes power a gut-wrenching hurt, teased by the wisp of hair you toy between your fingers and when the strap slips, from the silk of your shoulder, in an ecstasy fit to burst with the taste of you, I am a shipwreck lost in the depths of you 'til I find a harbour, deep and safe in the folds of you, my kind of love."

He took off his clothes and climbed in beside me and we lay there together.

Eventually we climbed out. Miles wrapped me in a warm towel and carried me to the bed. It felt like a wedding night.

Miles started reading again. A letter he wrote a few weeks after our last anniversary.

19. *"The Letter"*

Thank you for a wonderful anniversary. I remember it vividly. We arrive at the cottage in the early evening. I cook dinner – you know how I love to cook for you. Then we drink cold champagne. After dinner we bathe together in the little round tub. We dry ourselves then I carry you naked onto the bed. After four years together it should be stale, mechanical. But it's not.

It feels like the first time only better – much, much better.

I kiss your lips, then move down and kiss your neck, then move down and kiss your nipples, harder this time. Then move down and kiss your smooth belly. Then I move down further. Now I use my tongue. Sweet. So, so sweet, the taste of your arousal. And as you reach your hand down you can feel that I'm aroused too. But you knew that. You only need to fondle my side to make my flesh spasm with pleasure and very quickly give me a powerful erection.

Now I'm inside you. I look down at your beautiful face. Your eyes are closed. I lean forward and kiss your mouth. Tenderly. Then urgently. Then tenderly again. You open your eyes and look at me. You smile. The palm of your right hand pushes gently against my chest. I take your left hand and kiss your wedding ring. The thought that I'm making love to my wife moves it beyond the purely physical.

Having sex is such a stark little phrase. Making love sounds spiritual somehow. I can sense your breasts moving up and down as we make love, but I'm looking at your beautiful face. I lean forward and kiss you. More urgently this time. I brush your hair away from your eyes. You smile at me. I'm searching for a word. Holy. That's it, it feels holy. And that's not meant to be blasphemous.

Afterwards we lie naked on the bed and talk for hours. Everything, from favourite Beatles' songs, to the Sistine Chapel. How we loved Rome!

And the best thing of all? I haven't thought of any other woman since we got married. Why would I? I think of you all the time. And of course I'm thinking about you now.

With all my love
Miles

He was trying to make amends, but I couldn't make love to him tonight. I don't think he wanted to either. It was going to take time before we could trust each other again. I pretended to be asleep. Miles is snoring softly. Do I love him enough *not* to have his babies?

Day 14 – Sunday 6th October
10.23 am

I'm sulking. Feeling sorry for myself. I've told Miles I've got stomach pains. He's been really sweet, bringing me hot drinks and paracetamol. I'm lying on the sofa in a onesie, wrapped in a fleecy blanket. I have my emergency bar of Green and Black's in my pocket. The TV is on but I'm not watching it. Miles has gone out for a run and said he'll bring back the Sunday papers, and some chicken soup.

I can't believe how my feelings have changed. We discussed long and hard before we got married and I told him quite truthfully that after having such a traumatic time losing the baby, I didn't want to go through that ever again.

I remember the day we found out I was pregnant. Laurent had cycled to the pharmacy in the village to buy a test. Everyone would have known of course; you couldn't buy a loaf of bread without them knowing! When we saw the little blue line, Laurent gave out a big whoop, lifted me up and spun me round the kitchen. He had a smile on his face for days. He kept stroking my stomach and placing his ears next to my skin. "Can you feel anything yet?" he kept saying, day after day until eventually, yes, there was something, a fluttering and it was so exciting. He pinned the photo of the scan to his easel. He was inspired and strangely, I lost all inhibition. I posed in any way he asked, naked mostly, in the shade of the studio, skin glistening with sweat.

"I'll never sell these, Beth. Never," he would say, as he brushed and stroked the paint onto the canvas. Each stroke full of pride and love. He found my changing shape really sexy, and we made love over and over again, often outside in the meadow, surrounded by the smell of lavender. I thought life could never be happier than it was that summer in Uzes.

Then, one particularly humid, hot afternoon, when Laurent was gathering mushrooms for dinner and I was meant to be resting, I moved the bed. Our large, heavy marriage bed. I wanted it near the window, where the cool breeze could wash over me in the night. I tugged and pulled until it was halfway across the room. Later, when he came looking, he found me lying in a pool of blood on the floor. I remember nothing, except the pain.

It was Laurent who told me we had lost the baby, a girl, that I had almost died and that it was my fault. He went on a drinking binge that lasted two weeks, leaving me alone in the cottage for days on end. Maria looked after me, made wholesome soups and coaxed me to eat. Things gradually got better but I couldn't bear to have sex. Laurent got impatient, angry, kept blaming me for everything and was still drinking heavily. I came home one day and found him in bed with Maria. There was a huge row, and I tried to destroy the paintings, the reminders of what I had lost. I packed up and went to stay with Luce. I had nowhere else to go. I had no money and I was ill. One of the doctors I saw told me that it would have happened anyway, even if I hadn't moved the bed, but I never really believed her.

It took years for me to get anywhere back to having a normal life. Laurent had a wild time of course, for months he was never out of the newspapers, a new girl on his arm every time. He blocked our bank account and I had to fight through the courts to get enough to live on. And then I met Miles. My gorgeous, kind Miles and here I am, hurting myself, knowing he would never let me down.

11.25 pm

Didn't communicate much today. Miles kept out of my way, said he had work to do. I dozed off and on most of the time. Began to cheer up in the evening. Didn't need the chocolate! We watched Homeland together – new series - have missed Carrie Mathieson so much – I think Miles likes her as much as he likes Cersei Lannister!

At bedtime, he asked how the diary was going.

"Okay."

"Are you going to read a story tonight?"

"Hmm … No." I wasn't in the mood and I hadn't quite forgiven myself. "Well, maybe a funny one." I didn't want him to get too excited. "I've been trying to imagine what Muriel and Cedric get up to. Would you like to hear what I've written?"

"Not really, no." He turned over, switched off the light and closed his eyes.

I ignored him and began to read. He pretended that he wasn't listening, but I'm sure I heard a faint snigger before he fell asleep!

20. *"Cedric and Muriel (The Prequel)"*

Cedric moved back and forth faster and faster between Muriel's thighs. As he approached orgasm he looked past Muriel.
"I'm coming, dear" he said.
With a grunt he ejaculated inside Muriel. He leaned forward, kissed her on the forehead and rolled over onto his back.
"Did you come, dear?" he said.
"Yes, Cedric" lied Muriel.
"Well, goodnight then."

Muriel waited until he was snoring then crept to the bathroom. She shut the door and cleaned herself with a wet towel. Then

*she opened the wicker drawer. Reaching under the tubes of
makeup she pulled out her vibrator.*

*It was blue and soft like jelly. The batteries were in a separate
case, connected by a cable. She had put in fresh Duracells that
morning. She switched it on and turned the little wheel as far
as it would go. It made a high pitched hum, not loud enough
to wake up Cedric. The vibrator was stubby, only a couple of
inches long but that didn't bother Muriel.*

*She put down the toilet seat and sat back against the cistern.
She liked the coolness of the seat against her backside.*

*She spread her legs and ran a finger up her pussy lips. The
vibrator had little knobbles all over. With her left hand Muriel
pressed it hard against her clitoris and opened and closed her
thighs. With her right hand she pulled at her breast. Then she
opened her legs a little and slid her second finger into her wet
pussy and moved it back and forth, as if beckoning. The vibrator
and her finger squeezed together against her clitoris. She lifted
her right leg and placed her foot on the seat.*

*Her breathing came faster and deeper. She could feel orgasm
approaching. Making sure not to make any noise, she pressed
herself back against the cistern. As she came she arched her
back and shuddered. With eyes closed and mouth open, she
smiled with pleasure.*

*Then she rinsed the vibrator, put it back in the drawer and got
back into bed. She half wished that Cedric would walk into
the bathroom one night. She could imagine his shock:*

"What ARE you doing, dear?"

"Oh. Cedric, I'm masturbating. See?"

"Well, come back to bed."

"Yes, Cedric"

*When they were eating lunch the next day, Cedric said;
"Look, dear, I've been thinking. This sex business. I think it's
getting a bit stale – for me anyway. So I've been having a*

word with that Imogen friend of yours. She tells me they have
masked balls for adventurous people. It's about an hour from
here. I think we should buy a couple of masks and go."
"Whatever you say, Cedric" said Muriel.

Haha! That made me smile. Maybe the worst is past. Going to
sleep now.

Day 15 – Monday 7th October
8.12 am
Miles has left for work. Cup of tea on the bedside table.

Laurent's exhibition opens today.

Backlog of emails, including four from Luce and two from Imo.
Read Luce's first.

Number one: I am soooo … sorry about the photo Beth, I just
didn't think. Please forgive me …

Number two: Are you okay??? Please tell me it's okay I can't
live with myself …

Number three: I am mortified Beth please get in touch and
tell me it's okay …

Number four: I suppose you're still angry with me, are you never
going to speak to me again … I can't live with myself …

It's always ME ME ME with Luce. Was she always like that? Answer:
Yes! She'll never change and I should put her out of her misery!

Hi Luce,
It's ok. I forgive you. I was bloody angry at the time though

but it's all over now. I should never have lied to Miles. He's ok about it. You probably did us a favour! Sorry to run out on you like that. I did enjoy staying with you and I do appreciate you, really! The flights, the Ritz tea, the dinner all lovely. Can we forget about it? Love Beth x

She replied immediately.

Darling Bethie
So glad we're chums again. I was so upset after you left that I've decided to turn over a new leaf! I'm going to that group, the sex addicts anonymous thingy, and I'm going to try really hard to give up all my little 'boys'... Luv Luce xxxxxxxxxx
Ps Going to see the exhibition today, will report back!

It's always extremes with Luce, but I have a smile on my face – she'll never change, and I don't suppose I'd want her too!

Now for Imo's.

Number one: Hi Beth heard about Luce's faux pas. Hope you're ok. I'm here if you need me, Imo xx

Number Two: Hi Beth, let me know you're okay? Would you like me to come over? Imo xx

I replied.

Hi Imo
All is well, thank you. Sorry for not replying. I was really pissed off with Luce but I've forgiven her!! Miles understands – have told him. Should have taken your advice
Thanks for being there for me, Beth xx

Right, time for work!

10.39 am
Coffee time. Seems that Julie and Alex have hit it off. They are now officially an item! She is so caught up in her own life that she's forgotten to ask about our weekend. It seems ages ago now, what with London and all that.

Miles sent me a text

>>>Love you xxxx

Sometimes I feel I don't deserve him!

Students are full of questions after their reading week, panicking about the next hand-in. One of them asked about Laurent's exhibition. They'd noticed the poster. Was it worth seeing? I said they could make up their own minds when it comes in January. Wonder if Luce has been to see it yet?

Lunch
Stayed in the office to catch up with work. Big lecture on Wednesday – Neoclassicism – will have to update last year's PowerPoint.

Email from Luce.

Hi Bethy
At the Exhib. It's breathtaking. Everyone is wowing about it! Laurent is strutting about like a cock on heat, soaking up the admirers. He has a fan club, average age 14 by the looks of it! The portraits are stunning – they have given them a wall each with full lighting – sorry darling – they are rather explicit but you do have a gorgeous fanny!!! The press and TV are here too!

Don't get too upset sweetie! Love Luce xxxx

Oh God! Cocks don't go on heat... but I know what she means! And I've got a gorgeous fanny... for all the world to see. This is going to be so embarrassing. I'll have to leave my job!!

Can't concentrate. Keep seeing nudes and fannies everywhere, but most of them are sanitised versions!!

5.39 pm
Can't remember cycling home. Did it on automatic pilot. Surprised I didn't get knocked off my bike. Still upset at the thought of my fanny being on the ten o'clock news and in the weekend mags. With any luck, it'll be seen as being too explicit, but then again, they did print Freud's Kate Moss! I'm doomed!!

I need some distraction therapy. I'm going to bake.

7.39 pm
Poor Miles came home to find nothing for tea except cupcakes! He didn't mind and has nipped round to the Happy Valley for a Chinese. I don't know how to bring up the subject of the exhibition.

Midnight
Miles is asleep.

He came back with the food, waited until we had eaten and then he surprised me.

"I want to go and see the paintings, Beth. Will you come with me?"

I was speechless.

"I thought we could fly down on Friday night and stay over 'til Sunday. Can't afford first class though!"

I still couldn't answer. It had taken all my concentration just to eat the meal.

"I need to see them for myself Beth, and I want you to be there."

"Luce has seen them."

"And?"

"And what?"

"What did she think?"

"She said my gorgeous fanny was plastered over two walls of White Cube!!"

There was silence. I couldn't gauge his feelings. Was he upset? Annoyed? Jealous?

Then he burst out laughing!

"Well that's worth seeing!!"

I threw a crumpled napkin at his head.

"IT'S NOT FUNNY!"

He went all serious, and then burst out laughing again.

"Well I am a bit jealous that the world is getting to see something that should be for my eyes only, but it is 'art' after all."

"And what if you see Laurent?"

"I would quite like to meet him. Put a face to the reputation. Maybe I could get his autograph and sell it on eBay!

I threw another napkin at him. This time he was ready and caught it. He didn't seem threatened or jealous, but how will he feel when he sees the pregnant me and the 'madonna' portrait?

He asked if I had a story for bedtime. "And not another Cedric and Muriel!"

"What would you like?"

"Since we're being all cultured and talking about 'art' what

111

about something classic, old fashioned, no modern stuff, Dickens, The Brontes, Jane Austen."

"I don't think they wrote erotica, Miles!"

It was his turn to throw a napkin at me.

"Okay, I'll see what I have in my collection. Go get yourself in the mood!"

I read through Imo's file and found a few that seemed to fit the bill. Must ask her for some more. I decided on a period piece.

21. *"A Period Piece"*

After the death of her mother, Caroline was exposed to very few members of the male sex. Apart from her father, who more often than not stayed on at his club in the City, she saw only George the old gardener who had been with them since her father was a boy, and Mr Noyes, who came to teach piano twice weekly. Mr Noyes was a poor specimen who suffered from chronic congestion, only alleviated by constant expectoration and nose blowing. Caroline found him distasteful and abhorred his foul breath. She despaired of meeting any man equal to the dashing heroes she found in the pages of the penny novellas which she bribed Nellie, the parlour maid to bring from the village.

Day after day she sat in the garden and dreamt of being swept off her feet by a debonair suitor, and when her father arrived home late by the post chaise one cold Wednesday evening in late March, she hardly expected him to be accompanied by her cousin James, now a Captain in the King's Guards. Her last memory of James was of a delicate boy of ten, dressed in blue velvet, with an excruciating lisp and dreadful manners. Why, he had used his fish knife to eat the meat and had little idea of how to compose himself at luncheon. He spoke with his mouth full, pulled her ringlets and was generally uncouth. And now here he was, all 25 years old and full grown, standing six foot at least in the hall, magnificent in his uniform and knee-high leather boots.

He too, had only a vague memory of the spoilt six-year old, who had refused to play with him and insisted on correcting him at every opportunity, but James was now stunned into rapture by the beauty of the sweet young woman he saw before him. He could feel his member rise to attention at the very thought of kissing her pink lips, and he adjusted his sword to accommodate the new recruit.

Dinner was passed in a haze of desire. Caroline stared at his dark eyes and moist lips as he chatted nonsensically with her father about the Crimea, and felt a new and welcome stirring in her female parts. James was trying hard to contain his desire and with every flash of her perfectly small, pearl teeth and pink tongue licking the crumbs from her fingers, he felt he would lose control and expel his seed uncontrollably during dessert.

After dinner, her father declined cigars and port, repairing straight to bed on account of a headache, leaving the two young excitable cousins alone together in the drawing room. The door closed behind them and we may never have known what happened next if Nellie the parlour maid had not chosen to peek through the keyhole.

The vision she saw framed by the wood was enough to make her swoon. The fire was burning brightly and she could see Caroline's face glow in the red light. Shadows flickered across the white tulle dress as James took her masterfully in his strong arms. His sword was obstructing his desire and he removed the leather belt from his waist and let it fall with a crash to the floor. Caroline flinched at the noise and he was enraptured by the flush of pink on her cheek. He longingly kissed her neck, sucking the skin to leave a faint trace of a passionate bruise and her breasts heaved and rose like two creamy mounds of freshly churned butter, soft and malleable under his firm hands. Caroline's eyes were closed and she looked ecstatic. She instinctively lowered her hands and stroked the bulge in his trousers. Nellie had to stuff the corner of the apron into her mouth to refrain from gasping out loud and alerting them to her presence.

Soon he had lowered her dress, slowly slipping the lace off her quivering shoulders, kissing and licking her skin as the beauty unfolded. Her bodice lay exposed and he ripped open the lace fastenings, one by one until her breasts were bare, brown and freckled like a sparrow's egg and nipples pert and dark as chocolate. He took them in his mouth and sucked long and hard. Caroline groaned and tightened her grip on his loins.

James pulled down the petticoat over her hips and ripped the fragile bloomers until he could push his fingers hard between her legs, feeling the soft down and rejoicing in the wetness he found there. Caroline unfastened his trousers and gripped the largeness, making it grow and pulse with every stroke and he made a small noise that made her laugh and he flung her on the ground and buried his head deep and licked her juices until she begged for mercy And just at the point when he was about to enter her, strong and sure, Nellie fainted and had to be carried to bed by the footman.

At breakfast next morning, Caroline's father was surprised by the lack of appetite shown by his daughter and her cousin and hoped they were not sickening for something.

114

Miles seemed to like this and asked if he could have a piece too. I was happy to oblige and now, dear diary, like the peeping maid, I think you have seen too much! It's off to sleep for me.

Day 16 – Tuesday 8th October
8.12 am

Miles is off to work. He was very subdued this morning. The press have released details of the inquiry. Seems Social Work had tried to get an injunction but it's been overruled. Just read about it on the iPad. There's a short video of Miles and Shonagh coming out of the courtroom. It was just as I had seen them. He has his arms around her shoulders and her face is buried in his chest. It's odd seeing another woman so physically close to him, and she is very attractive, which will please the newspapers. I'm still not comfortable with the idea of Miles having slept on her sofa. It's all very much in the public arena now, just like my portraits!

Going to visit Imo at lunch time – will bring her some cakes, there's far too many for us to eat – I got carried away!

10.37 am

Coffee time. The place is busy. There's a special outreach event with local schools. I'm hiding in my office. Julie came in to escape and we chatted about her latest romance. Is everybody obsessed with sex, I wonder? Haha, with that thought I got a lengthy email from Luce detailing her exploits with the fellow addicts!

> *Hiya Beth*
> *Just had to tell you about the SAA meeting … well not quite as upmarket as our sex therapist in Knightsbridge, but an office above Starbucks in Islington! Rob didn't want to come. He says he doesn't have a problem, so I went myself. I'm not a wallflower but even I felt a bit wary about walking in. But the woman who runs it, Mary Gladflower, reminded me so much of Imogen, motherly and*

very welcoming. Cups of tea were offered in polystyrene cups and seven 'addicts' sat in a circle facing each other. I have to say we all looked pretty ordinary. I dressed down deliberately, in jeans and sweater and no designer labels at all, Beth!

I thought it would be mostly men, but five were women. I was the only newcomer, so Mary asked the others to introduce themselves. They all started by saying, 'I am so and so and I am a sex addict.' I just said my name was Lucy!

We were all encouraged to speak. I waited until the end. I have to say it was hard to keep a straight face. I could have outrun most of them before breakfast! Philip, a middle-aged bus driver, wanted sex three times a day but could only climax if he had sex standing up. His wife hated this because she had a bad back, so Mary suggested they compromise. Why didn't he stand up and his wife bend doggy style, over the bed? He said he had never thought of this. I almost choked on my custard cream.

Susie was more exciting. She was a young beautician and fantasised about having sex almost every waking minute. She could have orgasms just painting lip gloss on a customer. She wasn't gay, she said, but she found women erotic. She particularly loved waxing bikini lines, especially doing a full Brazilian, and encouraged the customers to raise their legs over her shoulder so she could get better access to their labia. I was getting a bit wet at the thought! When she was with men, she had this desire to wax them too, especially around their testicles. She loved the feel of hairless balls, but they seemed put off by this. Peter suggested she stick to women.

The others seemed quite shy but Mary coaxed an elderly woman called Jennifer to say something about her problem. It turned out that Jennifer had never, ever been with a man, but had sex four times a day using a cucumber, a banana or other cylindrical fruit. She felt this wasn't healthy but I couldn't see what the problem was. I had used a peeled cucumber just the other week, and very good it was too! But Mary suggested a more rewarding solution was to buy a vibrator or sex toy from Anne Summers. I recommended the Rampant Rabbit and Jennifer was very grateful. I saw Mary taking notes.

When it came to my turn, I told them I had a fetish for threesomes and I could see a little excitement appearing in the crotch of the young man sitting opposite! Afterwards he slipped his phone number into my hand. Somehow, I didn't feel the meeting was achieving the desired purpose! I don't think I'll be going back again, but it was fun and I can't wait for my next Brazilian!

Seriously though, I have decided to make more of an effort with Rob. I think we should try twosomes for a while and see if we can rekindle some romance.

Hope all is going smoothly at your end sweetie,

    Love Luce xxx

Was that a joke? I never know when Luce is being serious, but she's reminded me I need to book an appointment with Gina before going to London. Confidence-wise I need to look my best.

Still trying to write tomorrow's lecture.

4.38 pm
Teaching over. Having a cup of tea and a bit of breathing space before heading home.

Cycled over to Imo's at lunch time. Lovely day. Sunny and very autumnal, burnt orange against a piercing, china-blue sky. A painter's delight.

Imo was pleased to see me, and the cakes.

"You must have been seriously upset Beth, to make so many!"

I told her about Luce's description of the exhibition.

"Does Miles know what the portraits are like?"

"Almost. He knows I'm naked."

"How did you get on with Laurent?"

"It was okay. He was charming. He looks great; despite the fact he's over fifty now, he hasn't changed really. Dinner was fun. Rob kept us all amused with his anecdotes; you know what he's like! Laurent offered to show me the paintings."

"Did you go? Just the two of you?"

"Yes."

"And?"

"They are amazing Imo. I'd forgotten how dramatic they were. I cried when I saw myself. The baby and all that. It just came flooding back. Laurent was crying too, and I actually felt sorry for him."

"Beth!"

"It's all right Imo. Nothing happened. We cuddled a bit and comforted each other but it was a lock up, not a bedroom! He got me a taxi back to Luce's. It was pointless going really, it just upset me and made him more determined than ever to put them on display."

"Did you tell Miles?"

"Not about the cuddle, no. It meant nothing. He wants to go down at the weekend and see them."

"Really? I'm surprised. I wonder what he'll think?"

I shrugged my shoulders. I had no idea how he would react.

"I'm just frightened by my own reactions, Imo. I feel so desperate for a baby. The need feels so terribly strong."

"That's understandable Beth. At the time, you pushed all those feelings aside and never really came to terms with your loss. You're still grieving for the baby you never had."

I started to cry. "I was going to call her Aimee. Today would have been her due date, the 8th October. She would've been ten years old."

Imo held me close until the tears stopped. "It's good that you're crying. It's not wrong to remember."

I felt better after that and we had more tea.

"What about Miles? Does he know how you're feeling?"

"No."

"Don't you think you should tell him?"

"He'll just get upset. He won't talk about it."

"Why is he so against having kids, Beth?"

"It's to do with his childhood and his job. I can't tell you why, because it's not my story to tell."

"Okay. So what happens now?"

"I don't know. I mean I could just 'forget' to take the pill, couldn't I? I'm sure other women have done that, but it would be deceitful and I couldn't live with myself knowing I'd tricked him into becoming a father. I love him so much Imo, but I want to have a baby too."

"As I said to you before Beth, it's all about communication. You have to talk to him."

"But I can't! I'm scared. If I tell him how I feel, I'm going to lose him. Before I met him, he'd lived with Judith for six years, and that's longer than we've been married Imo, and when she said she wanted a baby, he left her. What if he does that to me? I'll die, Imo."

"It's your choice Beth. You have to decide what's important to you."

I left feeling sad and confused. Had to rush back to college for afternoon class and only just got time now to think over what happened. I'm going to have to take things slowly. See what the weekend brings. His reaction to the paintings will decide I suppose. Need to get home, it's getting late.

7.30 pm
Miles is playing squash. I'm eating cheese on toast and watching a programme about Ancient Greece. Brings back memories of my gap year. I was supposed to meet up with friends for a job on an olive farm in Corinth but got waylaid in Paris and never quite made it. Waylaid for years ... Still have a passion for Greek myths and legends. My favourite Disney is Hercules!

Midnight
Miles is still up. He's typing stuff on the laptop. Something to do with work. He's been at it since he came home. He just grabbed a sandwich and went straight on to the computer. Says he'll be finished soon. I'm tired. I wanted to read him a story about Greek gods. I'll just have to read it to myself instead.

22. "Persephone and Pegasus"

He flew across the skies at the summons of Zeus; what would be his mission this sun-kissed Solstice day, he pondered.
"Persephone is sad, Pegasus, you must carry her to Mount Vista so that she can find a new love," Zeus decreed.
"You can be sure, Zeus, she will be safe with me. I will guide her through the stars on the long journey and we can rest along the way."
The beautiful creature bowed his head in deference to the daughter of Zeus as she mounted with ease and clung to the strong mane.
"Farewell, my father. When I return, I hope it will be in a

more mellow mood and perchance with a handsome god of strength and fortitude."

The wondrous horse sailed onward, his precious charge much cheered by the beauty of the planets, but even more so by the constant motion of the steed between her legs. More than thrice Persephone cried out in ecstasy as her womanliness reached its peak, much starved of affection as it had been for these past long times. Pegasus knew his power and writhed to her rhythm as in perfect harmony they continued their journey.

"Let us rest, Pegasus", she eventually suggested, "here upon this cloud bank where we have a perfect view of the mortals below in Athenia."

All the gods loved to look on the world of the mortals, rarely interfering, unless specifically requested and Persephone was content to gaze and watch them at their daily tasks.

"Who is that young and handsome boy who smiles so readily?" she asked.

Pegasus had untold knowledge of the mortals and knew this boy to be Portus, the son of Horatio, a great scholar of Athenia, so imparted this information to his Princess.

"Why must I choose a god to be my new love, why not a mortal?" Persephone asked. The joy of riding the back of Pegasus was still fresh in her mind and she had the image of a similar pleasure with this muscular Athenian vividly in mind.

"The wrath of Zeus is well chronicled and, as you are aware, no mortal is permitted to seek a liaison within our world." Pegasus caught the dreamlike expression on his charge's beautiful face and added:

"Hades is the penalty, Princess, eternal damnation."

A fleeting picture of the underworld flashed through her mind, hellfire and gargoyle creatures abounded there, she knew. Still the handsome boy enticed her and before Pegasus could inter-vene, Persephone stepped through, into the mortal world. There was nothing Pegasus could do now, unless specifically called upon by name.

As soon as Portus set eyes on Persephone, he was entranced, as she had planned. She led him to a deserted place and took him in an embrace. Never before had he experienced such passion in a woman. She tasted of nectar, her hair was like silk and she had skin of a softness he had only before imagined. Disrobed, they made love throughout many hours, when the boy eventually asked:

"From whence you came and what are you called?"

"I am Persephone, daughter of Zeus and I choose you for my love."

Portus was at once distraught and enraptured. He had never before seen such beauty or known a woman so aroused and willing, yet he too knew the penalty for laying with a goddess. She saw his distress and lifted her breasts for him to suckle and thrust his hand to her throbbing mound.

"I will call upon Pegasus to go to Zeus and bring him to see my happiness. When he sees how changed I am in aspect, he will surely welcome you as a mortal son."

Pegasus knew that Zeus would be enraged and that the blame would be laid upon himself, but such was his love for Persephone that he was willing to carry her message to the King regardless. Meanwhile Portus spent every waking hour with his goddess, marvelling at her need for him. She oiled his penis and slid it inside her, crying out with joy. No sooner had he recovered than she wanted him again, and again. The boy lay, exhausted, his head nestled between her thighs so that he could begin lapping away at her, on command, as soon as she awoke. Soon Portus could no longer satisfy her craving and in anger she cried out for the mighty Pegasus upon whose back she was in a constant state of orgasm. Pegasus heard her call and joyfully flew to scoop her away and back to the palace of Zeus.

"You have no need for concern, father. I have chosen my new love and he is no mortal; it is your trusty Pegasus who has vowed to care and nurture me for as long as time itself."

Zeus smiled. This had been his plan all along.

A constant state of orgasm … now that would be a fine thing. Maybe I can dream about it, on my own. Miles is still tapping away next door. Oh well.

Day 17 – Wednesday 9th October
8.11 am

Miles was really late coming to bed. Think it was around two o'clock. He seemed happy enough this morning though. Said he got the work finished anyway. Brought me tea – he never fails – and wished me luck in my presentation. Said there was a letter for me, from Australia. He's left it on the hall table.

10.35 am

Coffee time. Presentation went really well. I hate the big lecture hall, in front of the whole year group, but today didn't seem so bad. At least they laughed at my jokes and Alex the technician had made sure everything was working properly. I could see why Julie finds him so attractive. It helps to be well prepared. 'Fail to prepare and prepare to fail, Beth.' I had learned the hard way and never wanted to experience the embarrassment of an ill-prepared lecture ever again.

Just opened the letter. Australian postmark; had to be my father. I wanted to read it in peace.

Is the world conspiring against me? I mean, how bad is this? He's sent me a picture of a baby, his baby, well his and Dee's baby to be exact. It seems I have a brother. Called Flynn. What kind of a name is that? Flynn. How can I have a brother 31 years younger than myself? It's ridiculous.

Lunchtime
Walked over to Princes Street. Got a sandwich from M&S and went into Next for a baby card, wrapping paper and a couple of outfits. Back in the office. Julie is oohing and aahing over them – I've asked her to wrap them for me. Really don't want to be doing this, wrapping baby clothes. Wrote the card. Nice and simple. Will go to the Post Office on the way home. Couple of tutorials now.

6.32pm
Made macaroni and cheese. Comfort food. Waiting for Miles to come home. It's raining. Lying on the sofa listening to music on my iPod. Truly madly deeply. I'm stuck in the late 90 s. Aerosmith. I don't want to miss a thing. I'm singing along. I'm in my bedroom. It's 1998. Dad is downstairs, he's shouting at me to turn down the music; don't I know my mother is ill? Of course I know she's ill that's why I'm playing music, trying to escape. And then it was just him and me. Glad to leave home. Paris, Laurent, Uzes. The wedding. He didn't come He's old enough to be your father. Ha, that's a joke. Dee's young enough to be his daughter. Does he see the irony, I wonder? Australia wasn't far enough away, he said. I'm crying.

7.39 pm
Miles is organising dinner. I'd fallen asleep and didn't hear him come in. I woke when the phone rang. Miles answered it, thinking I was still asleep.

"Yes, fine. That's a pity, we were planning to go to London this weekend. Yes I know. Maybe next time. Give them our love. She's sleeping just now, had a long day by the looks of it. No, she hasn't been herself since she got back. Okay will do, take care, bye Mum."

11.28 pm

Miles has been so good to me tonight. I told him all about the letter. Showed him the photo. He cuddled up to me and kissed my wet cheeks.

"It's okay, don't cry. Don't let it upset you, Beth."

He poured some wine and we ate dinner cosied up on the sofa.

"My mother phoned. Wanted us down this weekend. Lindy, Geoff and the boys will be there. Told her we were going away."

"It's all happy families just now, isn't it!"

I knew that was cruel. His mum had a hard time, bringing them up and losing his brother. Miles sat up and looked at me.

"What's wrong Beth? You haven't been yourself since you came back. I know things got a bit mixed up but I thought we were over that. Your dad's letter was a shock but you haven't seen him since you were nineteen. He's a stranger to us. He's never been in our lives. I've never even met him."

Miles managed to cheer me up. He poured another of glass of wine and got out the boxed set. We watched Game of Thrones and Miles hugged and kissed me all the way through. I relaxed and tried to put things into perspective. We went to bed early and I began to read another story about Greek gods but only got as far as *Pericles stomped around the foothills of Mount Olympus bemoaning his inability to satisfy Diana,* when Miles whispered,

"Stop reading, Beth"

"Why?"

"Come here and I'll show you!"

We didn't need the rest of the story tonight. He made love to me so gently. I love the smell of him. The feel of him. He makes me feel safe. Do I need anything more? Why complicate things?

Day 18 – Thursday 10th October
8.11 am
Had a lovely sleep. Have woken up feeling much better. The sun is shining. Miles has left. I'm sipping my tea.

Text conversation with Miles:

> >>>Love you. Last night was wonderful. Fancy a movie tonight?
> >>>Love you too. Last night was fun :) what's on?
> >>>Sunshine on Leith is out
> >>>Great! pick me up from work? Get something to eat on the way?
> >>>Okay xxxx

That's cheered me up. Off to work now!

10.37 am
Coffee time. Julie treated everyone to a doughnut. She is happy! Just hope it works out for her. Told her Miles is picking me up from work later on, to go to the cinema. She tells me how lucky I am to have such a hot husband and asks if I've ever made out with him in the back row! I told her she needs to stop fantasising but I could see from her expression that she has definitely done certain things under cover of the projectionist!

I do forget how attractive he is. My turn to fantasise.

I send Miles a text.

> >>>Have you ever had sex in a cinema?
> >>>I am in a meeting. No!
> >>>Do you fancy it lol?
> >>>No.

Ha well, that was short and sweet! I suppose he is 34 years old and a respectable GP! I'm sure Luce has tried it! Don't dare ask her. Wonder how her life of abstinence is going. Should really tell her we'll be in London this weekend but Miles probably won't want to see them or get roped into Rob's drinking sessions.

Lunch
Easy day today. Just some repeat classes and a bit of revision. Walked over to park. Said hello to the ducks again. Little Freddy is still larking about! I gave him some of my very overpriced hummus and red pepper sandwich. I am sketching in the margins. Must get on with my drawing again.

5.00 pm
Just waiting for Miles to pick me up. Don't know why, but I feel excited, like I'm going on a first date!

Midnight
Had a great evening. Went to Wagamama. Had superb noodle soup. Managed to spill it all down my new blouse! Miles tried to wipe it off but just made my nipples stand to attention! He noticed and smiled.

Movie was great. Feel-good stuff. Really funny at times and then sad. Made Edinburgh look terrific. Came out of the cinema singing and embarrassed Miles! Some of the songs were new to me and when we got home I downloaded a few onto the iPod. Didn't try to have cinema sex with Miles. It was too busy!

We had a cup of decaf tea and went to bed. I do like a good movie. If we couldn't have cinema sex for real, then I would give Miles a sample of fiction!

23. "Kari's First Time"

Kari felt very self-conscious and hoped no-one would come in. She gingerly placed two one-pound coins into the machine and pressed the button. A satisfying plop dropped a small packet into the tray. She picked it up quickly and shoved it into her back pocket. Looking in the mirror, she detected a new expression, almost conspiratorial, and a soft flush spread across her freckled face. Smoothing her hair, she thought she looked good, and desirable. The family holiday in Ibiza had left her skin brown and glowing, and she was able to wear her legs bare under tiny, fashionably ripped shorts. The Hollister carrier bag had a naked man on the front and she felt herself getting wet already. Two guys in soft leather trousers and bare, toned chests had been offering free perfume sticks in the Mall. It seemed that everywhere she turned was sex, sex, sex. She felt ready.

Liam was waiting at Costa. Bang on time. She saw him from a distance, standing against a pillar trying to look casual in his grey Superdry hoodie and faded Levi jeans which had slipped a little down his hips to reveal the red waistband of Calvin Klein boxers. He looked hot and the muscles in Keri's stomach gave a lurch. He looked up and when he saw her approach, gave her a beaming smile. His eyes followed her tanned legs, the shorts riding up her thighs and the cropped pink top, stretched over pert breasts and revealing a flat, brown midriff. He imagined licking her navel. This was a dangerous thought which immediately gave him an erection and he was grateful for the roomy crotch of his jeans. She came up and pecked him on the cheek.

"Hi babes," he said and threw his arms round her shoulders. She smelled of vanilla and musk.
"Hi lover boy," she replied, jokingly and snuggled into his

128

shoulder. She liked that he was a good bit taller than her and she felt the roughness of his stubble on her forehead. He was wearing the Hugo Boss cologne she had brought him back from her holiday. Kari was aching with desire.

"What's the plan? Any ideas?" he asked.

"Do you fancy the new James Bond movie?"

"Sure. Let's go."

They went upstairs to Cineworld and got seats right at the back. It was 11am on a Tuesday morning and the place was deserted apart from three teenage boys in the front row. Liam smiled. He knew they would be wanking off as soon as the picture started and the first semi naked female appeared on the screen. Kari and Liam settled down to watch the adverts. Liam moved his arm over her shoulders and stroked her neck, down to her breast and tucked his fingers inside her bra, finding a hard nipple. He rubbed it lightly and Kari began to moan a little. She turned to kiss him and his lips were wet and welcoming. The cinema was dark and warm. The ceiling lights twinkled and Kari enjoyed the feeling of plush seats skimming against her bare thighs. He pushed his tongue into her mouth and she felt the sharpness of his teeth against hers. The bulge in his jeans was growing and Kari squeezed her hands inside the waistband until she could feel the hair and flesh of his erection. He let out a low moan and she squeezed even harder. He pulled down the zip of her shorts and felt the wetness between her legs. Two fingers inside her and Kari could barely breathe. "You are so hot," he said.

"Mmmm..." Kari replied, kissing his neck and running her hand through his hair.

He flicked her bra strap and felt her breasts slide into his hand, soft and round. It was unbelievably nice. The movie was starting and the Bond theme was sounding in their ears. They could moan as much as they liked because no-one could hear.

Kari knelt down between the seats and took him into her mouth, long and slow she sucked until he came in spurts down her throat. She swallowed hard and giggled. He pulled her close until she was sitting astride him. He rubbed her with his thumb until she was writhing hard. He sucked her nipples and she pulled his hair tight in excitement. The drama on the screen was unfolding, Bond was being chased, guns were being fired. She felt him coming again, rising in good form. She pulled the packet from the back pocket of her jeans and waved it in front of his face. The foil flashed in the darkness. She could see a broad grin stretch over his face. Christmas had come early! She handed him the packet which he tore open with his teeth and, taking his hands from her for just a second, he slipped on the condom quickly before she pushed herself on top, taking him right inside as deep as he could go and she rocked back and forth until they came together in one almighty rush, just as Bond escaped his captors in a blaze of explosions and fireworks.

Kari snuggled into his chest, smelling his scent, then she turned onto her seat, sorted her clothes and said, 'Would you like some popcorn?'

"Ah the joys of condoms!" Miles started humming the James Bond theme and fell asleep fondling my nipples.

Day 19 – Friday 11th October
8.10am

Raining heavily. Miles was running late – he slept in! He's very tired these days, maybe I should back off a little. We both need a proper holiday. Greece would be good. Feeling anxious about London. We're both taking time off this afternoon to catch the 6pm flight. I'd better email Luce and let her know. It would be just our luck if we bumped into her! Miles has booked a nice hotel near the British Museum – pity we've missed Life and Death in Pompeii.

Hi Luce

Just a quick note to let you know that we're coming down for the weekend. Miles wants to see the paintings! Don't know if we'll have time to see you and Rob – we've booked a hotel in Bloomsbury. BTW my dad sent a photo of his new baby – seems I have a brother, called Flynn!

Talk soon

    Love Beth xx

10.34 am

Coffee time. Told Julie we're going to see Laurent's exhibition. She raised her eyebrows. She asked me to bring back a catalogue, signed, if you please! I hope she was joking. She suggested we take in a show, which is a good idea actually. Will take our minds off the exhibition. Dirty Dancing, Phantom (again!). Miles would prefer Book of Mormon probably! Worth a thought.

Email from Luce

Hi Bethy

That's wonderful darling. We must meet up; have dinner – why aren't you coming to stay with us? Can't wait to see your hunk of a husband!! That's pretty gross of your father, who wants a baby at his age??? Laurent's having a fancy dress party on Saturday night to celebrate. Imo's organising our outfits – why don't you and Miles come along, I'm sure she could kit you out with something fabulous and Laurent would be thrilled to see you again. You've been the talk of the town! See you soon sweetie!! Love Luce xxxxx.

… I've been the talk of the town … Oh God! And Miles absolutely hates fancy dress. It's his idea of hell. I did think about dressing up to excite him, as Imo suggested, but it would probably turn him off completely!! I don't think I'll mention it. Certainly not if it's Laurent's party.

2.00 pm

At home now. Managed to squeeze in a visit to Gina's salon. Completely smoothed and de-fuzzed but not the full Brazilian – don't want to scare Miles! Getting packed. Expecting him home soon. Don't know which clothes to bring. Better cover all eventualities I suppose. LBD etc.

Next day – Saturday 12th October
6am

In London, no problems so far. Uneventful flight. Arrived around 8pm last night. Miles dozed most of the way. Not quite the luxury of my last flight – just a cup of tea and a packet of shortbread! Used old Oyster cards to get the tube to Holborn. No private car with sexy driver this time. Brings back memories, being together in London again. We don't come back very often.

Miles has chosen a lovely boutique hotel, all polished wood and silky sheets. We decided just to eat downstairs in the hotel restaurant and sit in the bar afterwards. Meal was nice but predictable. Italian. Large platter of antipasti, Spaghetti alla Funghi, tiramisu, coffee. It was relaxing to be out together. Sitting in a bar, sipping wine, trying to avoid mentioning the exhibition. I wore a strapless back velvet dress and dusted my shoulders with sparkly stuff. Miles kept leaning forward and kissing my neck and running his hand up my legs. I'm sure the other residents thought I was a high class hooker! We were both quite drunk by the time we went upstairs. There was a bit of fumbling with the lights and Miles couldn't get the zip down on my dress. Neither could I! It was totally stuck. I had to come to bed wearing it – didn't want to rip it and I was too tired and drunk to fix things. We were giggling like school kids and fell asleep in a state of undress. Miles is still lying face down in his socks, boxer shorts and shirt. I have finally managed to get the dress off with a bit of effort and a pair of nail scissors. I'm naked now, going to cuddle up to Miles and see if he wants to play!

7am

Couldn't get Miles to rise to the occasion. That's happened a couple of times now. He seems willing enough, but brain and penis don't seem to be connected. Wonder if he's secretly worried about the exhibition. Maybe the thought of my nakedness being displayed to all and sundry is upsetting him. But it was an issue a couple of weeks ago too, when I started the diary, and he didn't know about the paintings then. Google says that stress is a factor … stress comes from how you respond to stressful events, not the events themselves. Men who have trouble talking about their feelings may find it hard to perform sexually… Communication is the key …

He's awake. I'll make us some hotel tea and read him a story. He enjoyed the one about the hypnotherapy session, maybe another one would help. Try to keep things light hearted, get a good start to the day, 'cos we're going to White Cube after breakfast, and I am totally dreading it.

24. *"Leonard and Angela's Second Hypnotherapy Session"*

Angela goes to see Leonard Laleham for her second session:
"I'd like to record our session today, Angela, I think it will help if I can listen to your fantasies a few times to help me understand the reasons behind your sexual desires; is that all right with you?"
"Oh, yes, Mr Laleham, anything you can suggest to help me would be good. It's so embarrassing for me when I bump into these people, as you can imagine."
"Right, recorder on, now same as before, Angela, just relax completely and listen to me count you down until you feel you're floating; one, two, three, four…
"I'm floating Mr Laleham."

133

"*Good. Now in your own time, tell me what's on your mind right now.*"

"*This morning I went into the bakery, it was early and Jo Pilsbury came over from out back to serve me, his hands all floury and pudgy. He told me he'd just finished putting the fresh cream into the vanilla slices but he still had all the meringues to fill. I bought some croissants and a cottage loaf which was still warm and hurried back home because I just couldn't wait to lay on my bed, close my eyes and start thinking about Mr Pilsbury and his cream meringues.*

"*First of all he's making dough. I know he's a tubby man and I don't usually like fat men but I see his chubby hands kneading the bread mixture 'til it's smooth; such a light touch he has, but strong too. My breasts ache for his touch, like two plump dough balls they are and I imagine his hands massaging my body until he reaches between my legs and begins to rub the lips between his sensitive fingers, as if he's rubbing butter and flour together. He coaxes my clitoris, not touching it, just rubbing fat fingers around it until I can take no more and he brings me to a raging climax.*"

Lennie is fascinated listening to Angela's vision of the local baker, an unremarkable man in every sense, and realises he will never again take his daily bread for granted. Angela continues: "*When Mr Pilsbury told me about filling meringues with fresh cream, it really got me thinking: one, because I love cream meringues but two, because it put the idea in my head that he has an enormous icing bag full of thick cream. I imagine him forcing the cream through, squeezing with those pudgy hands but instead of filling meringues, he's filling me with cream and slowly licking it away. He makes an exquisite job of twirls and curls and coronets as I hold myself open for him and then I wait 'til he leans down and licks it all off again. Then he lifts his apron and decorates his penis with a great swirl of double*

134

thick cream and pushes it inside me and it feels wonderful as he thrusts back and forth, back and forth and I squeal in squidgy delight."

She is silent for a moment and Lennie is speechless at the inventiveness of this demure young woman and wonders, not for the first time, what she will come out with next. Angela's quickened breathing subsides, as does Lennie's, and he admires the lovely line of her neck, a little clammy now.

"I like to visit the mobile library each Wednesday and I always try to get there around 12.30 when it's quiet and most people are at lunch. Jacinta is the new librarian and she is so exotic with her jewel coloured kaftans and henna in her hair. Some of the locals think they have to speak to her like she's a deaf person in case she can't understand them, but her English is better than mine! She told me she finds it really funny and sometimes puts on an Asian accent just to please them.

"Anyway, I really like Jacinta and sometimes I thumb through lots of books just so I have an excuse to look at her while she's replacing returned books to the shelves."

Leonard takes a deep breath. He never dreamt Angela may have lesbian tendencies as well.

"Carry on, Angela," he whispers.

"The last time I was in the mobile library, Jacinta took one of my hands and held it carefully. She told me I had beautiful hands and that I should make more of them with henna decorations, not just nail varnish. Her kaftan had quite a low scooped neckline and as she bent forward, I could see she had very pert, coffee-coloured breasts with surprisingly pink nipples. I thanked her and gathered the books up. I hurried off home and glanced round to see her on the steps of the mobile library, smiling at me. Well, I was wet before I even reached the house just thinking about the slender, brown librarian. I lay on my

135

bed and imagined her completely naked – slender legs, a fulsome bottom and those lovely pink-tipped breasts. She has a tray of henna dye and brushes and rather than my hands, she decides to decorate my body. She paints curlews and shapes, flowers and symbols, slowly drawing the different brushes over my body. She begins at the neck and works downwards towards my nipples which she gives a little pinch to make them sit up. Jacinta carries on downwards, making patterns on my tummy, then between my thighs with gentle strokes of red henna until I'm virtually covered in hieroglyphics. She massages my feet, decorating each toe with garlands, then slowly, she works her way back up my legs. When she reaches the curly triangle of hair, I part my legs and with one hand she opens the lips, just a little, while twirling the small brush around the folds. When she finds what she is seeking, the brush does its work, like a flicking, insistent tongue and I shout out loudly in ecstasy."

Lenny is not quite sure whether Angela has had an orgasm whilst she is telling him the fantasy, such is the sweat on her brow. He is sure, however, that he has.
"Ok, Angela, when I snap my fingers…"

When I got to the bit about the henna painting and the brush, Miles said he was going for a shower. Maybe not such a good choice after all. Stupid stupid me.

Midnight
An eventful day. It seems such a long time since Miles and I had breakfast and tried to pretend that today was just a normal day. We said very little and neither of us had much appetite. We decided to walk because the sun was shining and we needed fresh air after the stuffy heat of the hotel. The familiarity of the streets was overshadowed by trepidation and I clung to Miles' hand as if I were a child being led to her first day at school.

As we approached the entrance of White Cube gallery, I ran out of bravery.

"I'm sorry Miles, but I can't go in. I just can't face it."

"Are you sure? Do you want to go somewhere else? We could come back later?"

"No, we're here now. Why don't you go? After all, I know what they look like. There's a little cafe round the corner, I think it's called 'Muffin'. I'll have a coffee and wait for you there."

Miles reluctantly agreed. I gave a sigh of relief. At least I wouldn't have to see his reaction first hand. I walked round to the cafe and discovered that it's now a mobile phone shop. Rather than hang about, I decided to walk back and have a look at some of the other exhibitions.

The gallery was already very busy and I couldn't resist following the signs to Laurent's space. A glamorous blonde with a French accent was handing out glasses of bubbly and selling expensive catalogues. I had dressed down, deliberately, in jeans and a leather jacket but there was no mistaking her recognition.

"Monsieur Fournier is signing copies if you wish, Madame."

Laurent was there. I didn't think it could get any worse. Miles was going to meet him then.

The first paintings on display were those of Uzes, the big house, with its worn shutters, the cottage studio where we spent hundreds of hours, the sunflowers, the shimmering heat on the meadows, lavender fields. Beautiful and evocative. Then came the portraits. I could feel my heart racing. As Luce said, they were prominently displayed, well lit. I could see Laurent and Miles. They had their backs to me and were having an animated discussion. Laurent is tall, taller than Miles and was wearing his usual work outfit of crushed white shirt and even more crushed linen trousers. He put

137

his arm around Miles' shoulder and led him towards the paintings, gesticulating with his other arm. All very much blokes together. I felt so humiliated. So exposed.

Before they could see me, I turned and walked out of the building. I just kept walking and walking. My phone buzzed incessantly, but I couldn't answer. I knew it would be Miles. As I walked the streets, I thought of the two of them, standing there. I had expected them to be rivals, lock horns and all that. To see them so chummy was a bit of a jolt. Of course Laurent is a charmer and Miles can be easily led. It set my mind to thinking how similar they were in many ways; the intensity of their love, my love for them. To have loved two men so passionately was surely a wonderful thing. As I sit here and write I have to admit that both men had swept me off my feet.

I fell in love with Miles, properly, in Morocco. North Africa, tinged with exotic imagery. Kasbahs, Rick's Bar, Berbers and Ali Ba Ba's. Souks, Tajine and Couscous, Thuja wood and Kelims, Mosques, Medinas, Mogador and Marrakesh. Sunshine and clean, clean air unpolluted on the Atlantic coast, windy so the palm trees clatter and the Hitchcock gulls surf the breeze above the fish gutters on Essaouira's Skala du Port. Unlike the rude and noisy sea birds, we took our pick from the eager fish grills, moving crabs, white fish, lobsters and silver sardines by the boat load. Giggling, biting into the shark wondering if we'd the jaws for it, all served at the communal sunlit table with a plastic cover and cheap tin forks, illegal wine siphoned into green Fanta bottles and a simple salad of onions and red tomatoes oiled up to slip down with the barbecued fish. I flirted with the young fisherman come waiter and slipped him some extra Dirham as he led me to the stand pipe to wash my hands. I stooped smiling to splash the silver sunny water, a Nokia moment, if Miles had had one.

Back in the hotel, while Miles stashed the wooden trinkets he had bartered for and the rug I had begged for, I took a shower. When I emerged, dust free and glistening damp without the Sofitel white towelling robe, Miles stopped what he was doing. He said he loved the look of me naked and that the little shimmering beads of shower water had given me a diamond sparkle. He walked over, took hold of my hands and coaxed me gently to the large French bed. Such beds seem to have featured largely in my life. My suntanned body followed his lead but as he tried to pull me down towards him, I skipped away and ran out to the balcony that overlooked the long beach below. Miles followed kicking off his espadrilles and the loose dark blue linen chinos. He came up to me from behind and slipped his hands around me, gently cupping my white breasts, nipples like cherry stones pressed against his palms.

"People will see you," he said softly in my ear as though he didn't care if they did.

"Let them," I replied. He kissed the nape of my neck at that part where the spine is closest to the brain and even though he couldn't see it, I closed my eyes. It seemed the most natural thing in the world taking me from behind and I loved every stunning moment of it on that balcony above the long beach. We made love in equal measure, neither being selfish but both being greedy in roughly the same proportion so that neither of us felt the slightest bit let down. No one saw a thing. Anyone within ear shot could have heard, even though at the climax Miles clamped his hand, precisely but nicely, over my mouth to muffle my excited pleasure. He just bit his lip. We giggled about our al fresco episode that evening in the restaurant as we drank and planned the rest of our lives together.

Laurent's proposal, in contrast, took place in Nimes, many years before. He gave me the ring, in the ring, down on one knee like a moonlit Matador. Perhaps I should have read the signs, but I was young, very young and I just tossed my pretty head and kissed him hard in the white dust of the arena.

Our hotel, just off the Roman amphitheatre was where the bullfighters stayed. Its small reception full of posters of men with the same strong looks as Laurent, dressed to kill. The thin walls of our room couldn't hide our noise and we behaved without reserve, giving and receiving, so that at le petit dejeuner, we wore the blame proudly, when people spoke behind their hands or shook Le Monde even more than it deserved. We would have stayed in the room if the hotel had let us, but bullfighters don't tend to take their breakfast in bed.

They killed six that day and I leapt each time like the bull taking the coup de grace, jolted by the final lunge, the killer's sword in the beast. I had squeezed Laurent's hand so hard, it went white with lack of blood as each horned warrior had succumbed and been dragged as dead meat through the sand and dirt leaving a red scar as the Corrida band struck up with their brassy notes. The arrogant victor strutted his stuff like a caped crusader with a dead bull's ear held high in the air as a salute to the crowd. Perhaps the blood was a portent of things to come.

That evening after all the crowds had gone home, we slipped back into the arena, past the inattentive attendants and right out into the dim ring. I shivered in the cooler night air surrounded by the Roman stone lit in part by the dappled street lights and the more distant moon. Laurent shuddered too and put his arm around my bare shoulders to keep us both from the ghosts, keep us both together.
"How many have died here?"
"All in the name of love." Laurent replied quietly.
"Love?" I questioned.

"Love of the sport, of the spectacle."

We strode together as one, joined at the shoulders, kicking through the sand like a two-headed beast. Suddenly he turned and kissed me and our two bodies swayed, not certain which way to go. He fell down at my feet on one knee and produced the ring and I stooped and kissed him hard as we crumpled into a heap somewhere in the middle of the arena. Laurent's reluctant tongue found mine and his big hands, gentle as a giant's, felt for my smooth skin and made me feel almost sick with wanting more. I led him on, forced his touch beneath my skirts, those Spanish folds I had worn for the bulls, and up to where my thighs were taut. Laurent had the sure, strong, sensitive, nimble fingers of an artist, no hint of roughness. Big and bold, but smooth and slow. I knew they were magnificent, felt their magic; manipulative magic magnificence in that bullring in Nimes.

Had they recognised themselves, Miles and Laurent, when they met in the gallery without the secret handshake, wink and knowing nod? Had they bonded in that moment when they came together uneasily, questioning, not like fighting cocks with sharpened spurs ready for the blood, but rather like two lost schoolboys?

"You've caught her well." Miles would say.

"She was a willing and beautiful muse." Laurent would reply.

Anyways, it's all daydreams and water under the bridge now. After I left the gallery and walked for over an hour, I found myself outside Luce's house. I had been wandering subconsciously through familiar streets, and it was Imo who opened the door.

"My goodness, Beth! What a surprise. You look awful; what on earth has happened?"

I fell into her arms and burst into tears. She half-carried me inside. The normally pristine lounge was strewn with fancy dress outfits and Luce was dressed as Bo-Peep. It was surreal. Within seconds I had a glass of brandy in my hands and two friends fussing over me.

"I suppose you'd better answer your phone, Beth." It had been ringing non-stop for ages and Imo was right. I needed to let Miles know I was safe.

"Beth. Where are you? We couldn't find the cafe."

"We?"

"Laurent came with me. Where are you?"

He was with Laurent. They'd obviously been getting on like a house on fire. Perhaps comparing notes on my nudity.

"I'm at Luce's. And Imo's here too."

"Thank God you're okay. I was so worried." He paused for a male thought. "But if you're with your chums you won't mind if I stay on for a few drinks then?"

For an educated man, he had no insight whatsoever.

"No Miles I don't mind. Have fun." I hung up.

"Right girls. What outfit shall we get Bethy?" Luce could always turn a crisis into a farce! It was impossible to stay miserable for long with these two around. They insisted that, like Cinderella, I was going to the ball!

Laurent had taken rooms at The Carlton and they were hosting the fancy dress party. After much fun and games, and Imo suggesting I go as Salome and give them a run for their money, I eventually settled for a rather sexy Venetian Donna complete with mask and large beauty spot on my left breast. Luce changed out of Bo-Peep and into an Arabian princess. Imo decided on Fairy Godmother complete with wand. If only.

Rob's driver, Jules, drove us there and Luce flirted mercilessly with him. There was no sign of her reformed character nor her husband. He was going to join us later.

Reflecting on today's events I can't help feeling how much like a betrothal it seemed; the girls together, slowly getting sloshed, laughing and dressing up. The boys off on a pub crawl and all of us destined to meet up in a great celebration. Only it didn't quite work out like that.

The party was in full swing when we arrived. Laurent was welcoming everyone and was very drunk. Dressed as a Matador. How spooky was that! And like a matador he stalked me around the room.

"Very Venice," he slurred.

"Full of bull," I replied with a sweet smile.

"Beth. You are always the prettiest girl in the room."

It was difficult to know if my ex was speaking the truth but I liked what he was suggesting. He carried on moving his face closer to mine.

"I do miss you Beth. You were the best thing that ever happened to me. I don't know what you see in Miles."

"Miles is twice the man you will ever be, Laurent." I snapped back in my husband's defence.

"Twice the man, aye? But he won't give you the children you deserve." His statement hit me like a spicy bloody Mary in the face.

"You've been talking then?"

"We've been getting on like two old chums." Laurent crossed his fingers to indicate what he meant.

"Miles and I will work things out, Laurent. We love each other and we'll …work things out." I really didn't want to be having this discussion but I found myself in the grip of the matador and he whispered into my Venetian ear.

"Beth. Darling. I know we had some wonderful times together. Too brief, too tragic. But life has moved on and I realise how much I miss you. I want you back; want to have children with you want you as a part of my life once again." I pulled away from his grip.

"Never go back!" I said to him.

"Never say never!" he replied. "When I come up for my show in Edinburgh I want you to choose one of the paintings, one of your paintings and I want you to have it as a gift, a token of my love for you." I looked incredulous. He went on.

"If you think anything of me you'll accept it and I'll know then that, just maybe, there's a glimmer of hope, a place in your heart for me. If you don't I'll never see you again."

And with that he kissed me on my powdered but red cheek and staggered off to find more alcohol.

Rob was equally plastered as an Arabian sheik – obviously he and Luce had communicated at some point. Eventually, I found Miles propping up the bar, dressed as a Maharaja and chatting to a werewolf. Could have been male or female. Hard to tell. I stayed behind the mask just observing, then I put on a very bad accent and pretended to proposition him.

"Sorry love, I'm not available." He waved his wedding ring in my face.

"I've got a very beautiful wife and her fanny is plastered all over an art gallery!"

"Vereey funneey."

"No it's true. How's a man to feel when his wife's starkers. How's a man to feel, eh?"

"I don't know Miles. How do you feel?"

He realised then it was me.

"Beth?"

"How do you feel, Miles?"

"I don't know, Beth. I don't know."

He was already very drunk. The chance of a serious conversation was unlikely. Anything said would be forgotten by morning. Rob came and joined us so I left them together at the bar and went to join the girls on the dance floor. I thought I may as well enjoy myself after such a miserable day.

For the rest of the evening I made sure to avoid Laurent. He spent much of the evening wrapped around the very pretty blonde girl from the gallery. By eleven o'clock Miles was pretty far gone and I felt it was time to leave. We said our goodbyes and headed downstairs to call a taxi back to the hotel. About four steps from the bottom of the staircase, Miles fell and landed heavily on the polished marble tiles. I heard a crack and he let out a groan. I'm no medic but it was obvious he had broken his arm. The bone lay all crooked. They called an ambulance. There was much fussing and faffing about until, finally, a rather annoyed Venetian Donna and a rather teary Maharaja set off for A&E.

And this is why I am writing my diary in the exciting ambience of Guy's and St Thomas' Emergency ward. The registrar knew Miles and fell about laughing. Since he was so drunk, they decided to let him sleep it off before resetting the break. So I went back to the hotel, changed into more appropriate clothes and got jeans and t-shirt for Miles so he wouldn't have to stay dressed as a Maharaja. What fun! Here I am, watching Miles sleeping in a hospital bed, in the company of other Saturday night revellers and fed-up relatives sipping disgusting coffee from the vending machines.

Day 21 – Sunday Morning – 13th October
2 am
Miles has been to X-Ray and they've reset the bone. He is now being taken by wheelchair to the plaster room. What a bore. I have read my way through the exciting collection of hospital magazines. I wonder if they know that someone has left porny mags in amongst the ten year-old Car Traders and Homes and Gardens. It's been very entertaining. Some of the photo shoots are painfully reminiscent of my portraits. Was it disrespectful to

my pregnant body, to my baby, to have posed in such an overtly sexual way? Tiredness is confusing my thoughts. I shouldn't try to over-analyse things. I still don't know what Miles is thinking about it all. Maybe he thought they were great! There'll be plenty of time to speak about it later today. Meanwhile, I'll continue reading the porny mags. One of them has a very touching serial about two film-stars called Angie and Tim. It's kept me amused during the long wait! I feel like they are old friends. While nobody was looking, I've ripped out the pages and stuffed them into the diary. They say it'll be another hour before I can take Miles 'home' to the hotel, so I may as well keep reading to cheer myself up! It's been a rotten day.

PORN STAR 1

Tim

Tim's alarm clock went off. He groaned.
He drove to the studio, deadened by the thought of another day at work.
The cameras were already set up for the bedroom scene. The director walked over.
"Now Tim you've finished Cheryl's garden. She's made you a cup of tea and asked you to sort out the dripping tap upstairs. So now you fuck her, okay? Nothing fancy to start with, just straightforward in and out."
Tim nodded. He went behind a screen and got undressed. He walked into the bedroom set, blinking under the powerful arc lights. The actress playing Cheryl was already there. Naked, and on all fours waiting for Tim.
"Morning, Tim" she said turning her head "good weekend?"
"Yeah, not bad, Angie. You?"
"Okay, that's enough chat" said the director "let's get down to business. Okay Tim, you know what to do."

Tim turned around, and tugging a few times at his semi erect penis, gave himself a workable erection. He quickly slipped on a condom, turned around, climbed on the bed behind Angie and inserted himself inside her. She had already smeared KY jelly inside her vagina, so he slid in easily enough.

He fucked her hard, but without feeling, for a couple of minutes until she simulated a huge, screaming orgasm. Then he stopped. They both turned and looked at the director. He nodded and raised his thumb.

Tim worked for four hours. After a while he found it difficult to sustain an erection. The director was resourceful enough to ask him to perform cunnilingus on Angie. Bored and tired he licked her shaved vagina for a few minutes while she thrashed her head in exaggerated pleasure.

At 2pm he drove home. He poured himself a large whisky and slumped in the armchair. How had it come to this? How had his acting career fallen so far? He'd played Shakespeare, Shaw, Ibsen but for some reason the work had dried up and he was forced to make these wretched porn movies.

And for what? Straight to DVD and sold in sex shops or online. For lonely men to masturbate over? Or married men to hide and masturbate over while the wife was not around? Or perhaps for couples to watch together and try to spice-up their dulled marriages?

Angie was a nice enough girl. But Tim had no feelings for her. She was a colleague, and having sex with her was a job just like any other. At best it was mechanical.

Now with his wife, it had never been dull. They truly made love. And that was the difference. He loved his wife and that meant that sex was never dull or mechanical or repetitive. The act itself was the same as with Angie but completely different. They would lie together, entwined. He would be inside her, moving only a little but smiling at her beautiful face beneath him and she would smile back and he would whisper "I love you, Alison" and she would smile with delight and say "You do?" and he would smile and nod and lean forward and kiss her open mouth.

And after they had made love, they would lie side by side, naked, vulnerable and crushed with joy.

He would take her hand, bring it to his lips and gently kiss it. But she was gone now. Killed in a car crash. He thought of her all the time, except when he was working. That, he felt, would have been a betrayal. And he had to work. He had his little girl to look after. His motherless little girl.

PORN STAR II

Angie

My mother was a waste of space, but at least she gave me one good thing. Well, two good things really. Size 32GG boobs. I mean let's face it, I was never going to win prizes for my brains was I? And it was obvious from an early age that blokes spoke to my chest anyways. They weren't looking for conversation were they? So it was pretty easy for me to get into porno movies. Started at Jimbo's pole dancing club on the Esplanade and the rest is history, as they say in the trade.

I see myself as an actress first and foremost, and a dancer second. I mean, I'm not always naked. I do wear clothes from time to time and I get a few words to say. Why yesterday, we had a whole scene in the kitchen. I was making tea and Tim was sorting out the garden. I had at least three lines to learn. I reckon if I work hard enough, or screw the Director, I could make it onto EastEnders. Only joking!

    Tim is really sweet. Thing is, I fancy him like mad, but he's a professional. Never mixes work with pleasure, he says. God he is so hot. I mean, the whole widower thing, it just gets you right here. I get a lump in my throat when I see that look in his eyes. He's over me, his cock as big as a German sausage, giving me the old one two, in and out my fanny like a bloody fiddler's elbow, as my gran would say, and I'm getting so excited I could scream – no faking there – and there he is gazing into space, eyes like bloody cows. Empty. I bet he's thinking of his dead wife and I'm just like a lump of meat. I try and strike up a conversation, but he doesn't say much. Don't get me wrong. He's really polite. He's a real actor. He's done that Shakespeare on stage and everything. He kisses me real nice and soft on the lips, none of that tongue down the throat stuff that almost chokes you to death. Why do guys think that's a turn on? And then he sucks my nipples so gently, absent-mindedly, almost as if he forgets where he is, unlike somebody else I could mention who thinks he's trying to suck porridge through a bloody straw! And when he licks me down there … ooh … it's a dream come true. I'm getting a wet orgasm just thinking about it!

You see for me, this is a come up in life, but for Tim… well it's a bit of a come down isn't it? If it weren't for him needing money for his kid, and she is a cute little thing I have to say, he would never stoop to this, and that's why he'll never fancy me. And for the first time in my life I wish I had brains instead of boobs.

PORN STAR III

Tim

Filming started at 9.30 that morning. The director asked Angie and Tim to start with reverse cowgirl.
"You ride Tim and I'll shoot from the front so they get a good view of your pussy. Go for a couple of minutes then squeeze your tits and scream like you're coming. Okay?"
Tim groaned. Filming from the front meant that his penis

would be in full view as Angie rode up and down the shaft. He wasn't sure whether he could maintain an erection for more than thirty seconds.

It was as though his penis was no longer part of him. It was just an external appendage that he could screw on to shoot the scene and then remove once he'd finished.

Tim managed to stay hard for two minutes. Then the director gave a signal and Angie squeezed her breasts and jerked her head back and forth. She called out "yes. Oh yes" again and again.

The scene ended and the director moved to the next set up. This time Angie on top, face to face with Tim. The camera would be behind Tim's head shooting a close up of Angie's face and swinging breasts.

Tim was relieved. The angle meant that he would not need to penetrate Angie. But as the director shouted 'action' she took him in her right hand and slipped him inside her. It makes the scene more realistic, she said.

The scene ended and they stopped for coffee. Angie and Tim sat at a table with the director. As they drank their coffee the director instructed Angie on the best way to give a blow job.

"Well, I don't want to teach grandma to suck eggs" he said.

"Grandma? What sort of film are we making anyway?" said Angie.

"No, what I mean is …" he gave up.

Tim looked up at Angie and smiled. She's a nice girl, he thought. When she stops doing the porn movie pout and smiles. Too much make-up, though. And he wasn't keen on the fact that her vagina was completely bald. Full wax. Was that a porn movie convention, thought Tim? And did men really like it?

Angie smiled at Tim. Filming was a little easier for the rest of the morning.

PORN STAR IV

Angie

Felt really sorry for Tim today. I'm a bit miffed though, 'cos I obviously don't turn him on. He could hardly get it up – thought he was going to peg out on me! I don't usually enjoy the backwards cowgirl thing – I like seeing his face, but today I could sense he was miles away. He lost it completely for the next scene and I had to shove his wobbly dick inside me quick before Murrray noticed. At this rate he'll get the sack. I can't keep covering up for him.

I wonder what would turn him on? I asked a mate and he said some guys like a bit of fluff on the fanny. Maybe I should grow it a bit – wonder if Murray would mind. He did ask for the full Brazilian. And as for him, who does he think he is, trying to tell me my job. As if I didn't know how to give a decent blow. It's obvious he's never had a good one – he even mentioned his granny, weirdo!

Maybe that's the way to get Tim. I'll give him my best one –it's never gone wrong yet, and I've had plenty of practice – I just imagine I'm licking an ice cream cone, nice and slow, up and down and round the edges and over the top into that little holey bit, and then a nice big suck, full in – let them feel the back of your throat, and squeeze their balls, not too hard mind, finding that little squidgy bit that sends them crazy and then swallow the lot when they come! It's worth a try – Tim, you don't know what's coming!

And I'll do the full make-up just to be sure!

Tim

"Okay, cut" said Murray.

Tim stopped thrusting immediately and rolled off Angie.

"Tim" said Murray "at least try and look as though you're having a good time. "

"Sorry, Murray."

"Let's have lunch and we'll try again this afternoon."

Tim swung his legs over the bed and sat with his head in his hands. He felt exhausted. Not so much physically as spiritually. He was drinking more and his extremities seemed to fizz a little. Even his penis.

Kathy brought over his boxed lunch. A piece of fried chicken, a bread roll, a little packet of butter and an apple.

"Tim?" she said.

Tim looked up.

"Your lunch."

"Oh. Thanks Kathy"

They chatted for a minute or so. Tim sat naked but there was no embarrassment. Tim was very well endowed and Kathy looked down from time to time.

Murray came back in and prepared to shoot the scene again.

"Right. Let's get this one in the can. Tim, try and give it some. You're fucking this gorgeous woman. And Angie, try and say the dialogue this time. We paid good money for this script, you know."

"You mean – fuck me, stud. Oh, you're so big. Oh yes, yes" she said, slowly enunciating each word like a deliberate cliché of a great theatre actress.

"Okay, let's just shoot this turkey" said Murray wearily.

Tim and Angie climbed onto the bed and got into position.

152

Missionary, with Tim on top. Angie helped him to a decent erection, he slipped inside her and they both lay, looking at Murray waiting for instructions.

"Okay, you two. Action."

Tim began to thrust in and out of Angie. Angie began to moan in her synthetic, porn star way. Then she whispered "I think that Kathy likes you. And I know you like her. I know you won't admit it, even to yourself. But I can tell."

Murray made a circular motion with his hand meaning 'speed up'. Tim began to thrust harder and faster and Angie threw her head from side to side.

Then Tim slowed down, and took her head in his hands. He looked into her eyes and said "Really? Why would she want a messed up idiot like me?"

"Dunno" said Angie, smiling.

Tim carried on thrusting. Then he smiled at Angie, bent forward and kissed her on the mouth.

"You're quite a girl, Angie."

The scene ended. Murray was happy and called for a tea break. As Kathy brought the tea Tim covered himself with a towel.

"Thanks, Kathy. There's something I want to ask you. Would you go out with me? Will you be my girlfriend?"

"What?"

"Sorry. I sound about twelve. I haven't dated anyone since Alison."

"It's okay Tim. I'd love to" said Kathy kindly.

"Right" yelled Murray "let's get this last scene done. Angie, it's the blow job scene, so remember what I told you."

"Erm suck him like his grandma, wasn't it?"

"Something like that," Murray sighed.

Angie smiled. She loved to perform oral sex on men. And a man like Tim? Well she was going to enjoy this scene.

Panicked, Tim looked at Kathy, "Kathy, I can't do this. I'd be cheating on you. Right in front of you. I can't."

"Tim. It's your job. It's the last scene. We haven't been out yet. I'm not your girlfriend yet. It's okay. It's just one more scene. After all I've been watching you do her for the last fortnight."

The scene began. Angie knelt down in front of Tim and took him in her mouth. She began to suck, coaxing him hard. Tim looked up at Kathy and smiled. She smiled back. His cock swelled and stiffened. Angie sucked him expertly, winding her tongue around the head, lightly stroking his balls with her fingers. Tim stared into Kathy's eyes and did not shift his gaze. Kathy looked back, encouraging.

He felt the approach of a marvellous orgasm and came with a great spurt into Angie's mouth. Gratefully she swallowed his sperm. Tim stepped back, panting. He felt a little embarrassed as he looked down at her. But Angie was happily licking her lips. He looked up at Kathy, apologetically. She smiled as if to say 'it's fine.'

And Murray said "that was terrific. See you in a month for 'Plumber's Mate 2'."

PORN STAR VI

Angie

Well, let's face it. He was never going to fall for me, was he? Horses for courses, that's what my Uncle Jimmy always says. Got to be realistic. I mean I've seen the way Kathy's been looking at him the last few weeks. Totally smitten and the poor bugger couldn't even see it. So enter Mother bleeding Theresa. I'm my own worst enemy I am, but I just couldn't stand by and watch him mess things up. So I did my good deed for the day, more fool me.

We were doing a basic fuck, Murray being his usual charming self and criticising my acting skills – I've met his likes before, full of bullshit but secretly dying to get into your pants – and

Tim's doing his best but failing badly so I says to him while he's pumping away, that Kathy fancies you, you should ask her out. He comes over all shy like but, give him his due, after the magic of my blow job, he plucks up courage and asks her out. Not the best chat up line in the world, I have to say, but it works and she says yes.

Maybe I'll get my rewards in Heaven, but hey, every cloud and all that. I still get to fuck Tim on set, and things should improve pretty well in that department now that he seems to be getting his mojo back, and as for Murray, well I saw the way he looked at my blow job, only a matter of time girl, only a matter of time.

PORN STAR VII

Tim

Tim put his mobile back in his pocket.

"Sorry Kathy. That was Murray. He says 'Plumber's Mate' has been accepted. Now he wants me to do 'Plumber's Mate 2 – Dripping Pipes'. Thing is, I don't really want to. I've had this offer from the RSC and the other thing is, I'm with you now. It wouldn't seem right."

"Oh, Tim" said Kathy "I don't think you should. I mean I was turned on by watching you with Angie. Even though you weren't firing on all cylinders, I could see you were quite a man. But now? Well we've been going out now for a few weeks. It would be a bit weird."

"Good" said Tim relieved "that's settled. I won't do it. I'll tell him in the morning."

"Talking of morning. Do you want to stay here tonight?"

"Well, I haven't any pyjamas."

"No problem. You could borrow mine. Or... not."

"I'd love to, Kathy, but I'm not sure ..."

155

"Tim, we've been going out for more than three weeks. I think it would be okay now. You've taken things slowly and I'm glad you have. But our bodies are telling us the time is right. Well I know mine is."

"What are you saying?" he said playfully.

"I'm saying I want you to take me upstairs and make love to me. Bring the wine."

With that she took his hand and led him to her bedroom.

They kissed, a long passionate kiss and then undressed each other. Kathy lay on the bed invitingly. She parted her legs, just a little and Tim gasped. She was beautiful but not in the same way as his wife. She had soft ample breasts, her belly curved in sensuously and her pussy, with a light covering of soft downy hair, delighted Tim. His cock was fully erect. Smooth long and hard, all trace of his former problem gone.

He'd always loved cunnilingus. He bent down and started to lick Kathy in long upward strokes. Her pussy felt velvety on his tongue and he loved her taste and smell. Kathy reached down and rubbed her clitoris with two fingers. She moaned, not synthetically, but with pleasure as this man helped her to a full, joyous climax.

Tim's cock was now rampant as if it had been waiting a long, long time for this moment. He climbed on top of her. He wanted to look at Kathy's face and kiss her lips and whisper to her as he made love to her.

He pushed himself easily inside her and moved in and then out with long powerful strokes, lifting her head towards his so he could kiss her, brushing her hair away from her eyes so he could look deep into them, whispering to her, telling her that she was beautiful.

They came together as they knew they would, then lay on the bed side by side, Kathy happily stroking his hairy chest.

Tim poured two glasses of red wine. They clinked glasses and made a toast to Angie.

156

"I can't thank her enough" said Tim, "she knew before I did."
"Well, let's hope she meets someone nice soon. Perhaps on the sequel?"
Kathy put down her glass, slid down and began sucking gently on Tim's cock. He quickly became erect, as hard as before, and Kathy gave him a long, wonderful blow job. Tim smiled to himself. Even better than Angie, he thought.

PORN STAR VIII

Angie

Sad news and good news today. Kathy told me that Tim's been offered a proper acting job at last – Shakespeare no less – which means he won't be doing Murray's Plumber's Mate 2 anymore. I'll really miss him but I suppose it's for the best. Now that he and Kathy are an item it would've been a bit weird for her to watch him do stuff with me – although it could be a bit of a turn on, if you were so inclined! I asked her how they were getting on and she said fine with a big smile on her face. No problemos there then! I'm chuffed to bits for them, really I am. Couldn't have happened to nicer folk. Kathy says he'll get me tickets for his first production. Me and Shakespeare? No way José! But it was really sweet of her. Maybe I could sell them on! Anyways, true to form, Murray asked me up to his apartment for cock-tails – haha – and do you know what? For the first time in my life I said no to an offer. Yes, truly. I took a page out of Tim's book and said, thanks but no thanks, I don't mix business with pleasure! I'm a professional, I am. You should've seen the look on his face. I really wanted to say, go home saddo and wank off to one of your porno movies, but I need the job! I suppose he'll bring in Steve from the Agency, which is great. He's hung like a horse, as my mate Amanda would say, and he does give a great fuck, but only problem is he's as gay as a

157

nine bob note! Happy days! But you know, when you do sex for a living it kind of messes with your head and I'm pretty fed up with it to be honest. My roomie, Carmen, agrees with me so we're going to have a girls' night in – jammies on, couple of bottles of Lambrusco, a tub of Ben and Jerry's and The Notebook on the telly. What more does a girl need?

Indeed! I'm becoming quite attached to Angie! I was still laughing when they wheeled Miles through, looking sorry for himself. His right arm is in plaster and strapped up in a sling. There's going to be fun ahead. Miles is hopelessly right-handed. Apart from all the practical things, like eating and dressing, sex is going to be a challenge. It'll have to be girl on top for a while, maybe Angie's reverse cowgirl is worth looking into! That's assuming of course that he's still interested in my body after yesterday. Anyway, he'll be completely at my mercy for the next few days! It will also give me some time with my own thoughts. I have Laurent's proposal to think about after all...

Still Sunday
9 am
Got taxi back to hotel okay. Miles moaned all the way.

"Bloody, bloody stupid! Breaking my arm for God's sake! I'll be the laughing stock at work."

"You'll have a few days off though, won't you? Will you be allowed to drive?

"Don't see why not. It's only broken near the wrist."

"I don't know about that Miles. Are you sure the insurance will cover you?"

"Since when were you an expert? Even people without any bloody legs can drive!"

I went into a huff. I could see he was angry with himself and worried about work but anything I said was going to be wrong.

He's fallen asleep now, on the bed and I'm sitting here writing and thinking; we need to check out soon and get ourselves round to Luce's. I'd promised that we'd go there for breakfast and drop off the fancy dress costumes. Can't be bothered. Would just like to get home. Flight is at 3pm.

Still thinking about what Laurent said, about Miles not wanting kids. Laurent will pester me, especially now he's offered to give me a portrait. At the moment nothing in the world would take me away from Miles, but how will I feel in a month, or in a year, if no baby is on the agenda? Dare I talk to him about it? He hasn't mentioned the paintings at all.

Put on the telly. New information about Maddie. They've opened the case again. I don't fantasise about the joys of parenthood. It must be one worry after another. Gerry and Kate McCann have been to hell and back. You must worry every time your child goes out of sight.

3.30 pm
On the plane home.

Well, we managed to get ourselves over to Luce's for midmorning. Miles was apologetic in the taxi.

"I'm sorry Beth. Didn't mean to snap your head off earlier. Of course you're right about driving and all that. Need to make sure it's okay." He lay back and closed his eyes. I just stared out of the window, watching the busy traffic and feeling lonely

"Been in the wars, have yer?" The taxi driver was just trying to be friendly but Miles was not amused. When we got to Luce's, he stomped off and left me to pay. The driver shrugged his shoulders and gave me a sympathetic smile.

Luce was her usual ebullient self of course, dressed in a brightly flowered silk kimono.

"Rob's still asleep, poor thing! We had an argument about Russian prostitutes and I handcuffed him to the bed post!"

"As you do, Luce!" I said, in surprise.

"Tell you all about it later sweetie." She kissed my cheek. "Hope the broken arm isn't going to hold you back, Miles darling! Bloody

Marys anyone?" Miles asked for coffee with whisky which was not a good sign.

Luce insisted that Jules drive us to the airport and Miles slept the whole way. I dozed a bit too, in between watching Jules' smouldering eyes in the driver's mirror. I remember a very sexy taxi journey Miles and I had a few years ago. No sign of that today.

It took ages to get to the airport and we just made the check-in. Miles nabbed the window seat, even though he knows I prefer it. He ordered another whisky, took two painkillers and is now sitting with his head pressed against the window.

"It's not my fault you broke your arm Miles."

"Isn't it?" He closed his eyes and pretended to sleep.

So, he does blame me then, for Laurent, for the paintings, for him getting drunk …. Hmmm. The serious conversation is going to have wait until Miles is in a better frame of mind.

I'm going to read the rest of Lady Chatterley. I wonder if they have a happy ending?

Midnight

Miles is in bed. Sound asleep. He looks exhausted.

When we got home, I ordered a pizza and we just zonked out in front of the telly and watched *Homeland*; things are not going well for our two heroes, Carrie and Brody … quite a depressing storyline, to top off our rather awful weekend.

At bedtime I tried to lighten things up a little by reminding Miles of that sexy taxi ride …

> *We were both drunk from the party. You were kissing me, hard, in the back of the taxi.*
> *"How long before we get home?"*

"About twenty minutes," I said, "why?"

"Because I need to fuck you now, Mrs Rogers, right now."

I touched your crotch. "Yes you do" I said.

Then you said, "Stop the taxi. Yes, right here."

The driver pulled over and stopped. We were next to an industrial estate.

We got out. You handed the driver thirty pounds. "There're thirty more if you wait for us for a few minutes."

We found a place where no one could see. We were standing next to a black Mondeo. You kissed me, even harder now. Then, without warning you spun me round and pushed me down against the bonnet of the car.

As I braced myself on my hands I heard you undo your trousers and let them fall to the floor.

Then you lifted my skirt. You didn't even take my knickers off, just pulled them to one side revealing my very wet pussy to you. My legs were closed, but it didn't matter, you slid easily inside. Then I heard something tear and realised you'd ripped off my knickers. You eased my legs apart and pushed even further inside me. God, you were huge and you were fucking me so hard. You were like a wild beast, but I loved it because you were my wild beast. Then I heard someone shout "I'm coming. I'm coming" and realised it was me.

I came hard and heavy and seconds later heard you groan and pumped me full of your warm creamy sperm. Millions of little Miles' inside me.

You lifted up my head, bent round and kissed the front of my neck, breathless.

Then we got dressed. Well, you did. My knickers were ripped apart so I left them there.

We got back into the taxi, giggling like schoolchildren. As I got in I lifted my skirt. The leather felt cool and pleasant against my naked bottom.

When we got home you gave the driver a good tip.

I did too. I said "have you got a towel? The back seat's a little wet."

Miles, you are a wonderful lover – passionate, romantic, caring, tender, unselfish. I feel sometimes that my pleasure is more important to you than yours. Or rather that giving me pleasure brings you joy.

Making love to you is like a Mozart piano concerto. Full of warmth, exquisite melodies, sinuous textures, slow movements, faster movements and of course a wonderful and satisfying climax.

But sometimes it's like a Rolling Stones' song; "Honky Tonk Woman" perhaps. Short, urgent, a little rough, slightly off key, still satisfying, though.

"What planet are you on Beth? Do you really think I'm in the mood for anything right now?" He turned his back and went to sleep, broken arm resting outside the duvet. He didn't see the tears in my eyes.

What lies ahead for us, I wonder?

Day 22 – Monday 14th October
8.15 am
Had a huge row with Miles this morning. What a start to the week.

"You are so stubborn! Why can't you take the day off and get yourself sorted out like a normal person would? Phone the car insurance, see if they'll cover a driver or something. You look awful."

"I've got a full surgery of patients to see. What do you want me to do? Cancel? Can't expect colleagues to cover a drunken escapade can I?"

"It was an accident Miles. What if you'd hurt yourself hill climbing or playing squash?"

"Huh! Hardly the same is it? Look, I haven't got time to argue. I'm taking the bike."

And off he went. The stubborn idiot on his bike. Today I could just scream at him.

10.30
Coffee time. Cycled to work as usual and wondered how he could manage with his arm in plaster. Julie wanted to know how we got on at the exhibition.

"It was awful! Couldn't have been worse actually."

"What happened? What did Miles say?"

"Nothing. He's said nothing and that's what makes it worse. He went drinking with Laurent. Bosom pals and all that, then he got blinding drunk at Laurent's fancy dress party, fell downstairs, broke his arm and we spent four hours in A&E. He's now barely speaking to me."

"Oh God Beth, that sounds awful! Is he angry about the paintings or the broken arm?"

"He's angry about everything, Julie. Anything I say he snaps my head off."

"Well, you can sympathise with him, I suppose. It can't be easy and now a broken arm. Is he off work?"

"No. He cycled this morning, and I don't sympathise with him. He should've known better than go drinking with Laurent. I didn't even want them to meet – my worst nightmare – let alone go boozing together. Laurent borders on alcoholic, Miles could never keep up."

"How was Laurent, the paintings?"

"He was his usual charming self. The Uzes paintings were superb of course and he wants to give me one of the portraits. "

"Wow! That'll be worth a fair bit I should imagine."

"I don't know, Julie. I mean, what on earth would I do with it? I could hardly hang it on the living room wall, could I?"

"You could donate it to the National Gallery!!"

"Yeah, right! And have all of Edinburgh staring at my fanny! No thanks."

"It's a generous gesture, though."

"Hmm… I'm sure it comes with conditions and expectations."

"But he knows you're happy with Miles. Nothing could change that."

"I don't know, Julie. Things I used to feel certain about just don't see seem right any more."

"Such as?"

"Life, the universe and all that!!"

I don't normally bare my soul to Julie, professional relationships etcetera, and I certainly didn't want to be discussing my changing views on motherhood with the office gossip.

Class waiting. We've moved on to the Surrealists – fits in with my disjointed mood.

4pm

Worked through lunch marking essays and had a tutorial all afternoon. Feeling lousy. Depressed. Thought Milles might have texted but nothing.

Email from Luce – that'll cheer me up I'm sure. Not.

> Hi Bethy
> How's it going darling? That was a great weekend wasn't it? Have you recovered? Poor Miles – a broken arm. That'll cramp his style – you'll have to take the initiative in bed sweetie!! Rob is still recovering and Laurent has been round, moping about, waxing lyrical about your charms. I said he should've thought about that before you split up.
> I've decided to try monogamy for a while … give Rob all my attention, once I've finished things with Jerry… (and *Jules, Luce!*) … here's my little naughtiness about the Russian prostitute … enjoy!!!
> Luv Luce xxxx

Oh dear, yet another of Luce's stories. Well let's see if it can bring a smile to my face. I need all the help I can get today.

The fancy dress party …

"So about this Russian hooker?" asked Rob, as Derek lit up.

"There are fucks and there are fucks" said Derek as he expelled a cloud of blue smoke into the night air. "If you've never tried a Russian you haven't lived. There seems to be something about their years of suppression that makes the girls behave as though you are somehow liberating them, cutting off the yoke of strict state supervision and letting them free."

"Bloody hell!" said Rob.

"Tanya is a goer. There's nothing she won't do for me and I reckon she's the best bit of fun I've ever had…and I've had plenty," he added just for good measure.

"So could I get to sleep with a Russian girl?" asked Rob with genuine but hazy interest.

"Sleep dear boy! Sleep!" said Derek too loudly. "The last thing you'll want to do is sleep my old friend! These girls fuck like tigers! They're at you all night so you'll want at least three shredded wheat for breakfast that morning!"

"Bloody hell!" said Rob.

"Listen. I'll fix it up for you. Let me know when you want a night away in town and I'll sort it out for you. You'll need say five hundred notes, they like the cash, plus the cost of a good night out and your hotel and I can promise you the time of your life."

"Bloody hell!" said Rob. "I've always fancied a young Russian prostitute so I might well take you up on this one Derek. Thanks mate. Yes I will!" The night air caught up with Rob's lungs and his world spun a little more that it had previously. The idea of a feisty Russian girl beneath him or on top or in fact anywhere in close naked proximity was an image that he liked and he turned to go back into the village hall.

"Hello Rob." said Lucinda.

"How long have you been here?" he asked, with some confused concern.

"Long enough," said Lucinda. "I think it's probably time we went home."

The journey back home was frosty. Rob nodded off and Lucinda fumed on the back seat next to him.

"No much of a sheik tonight is he?" said the Scottish taxi driver as he observed the Arab slouched against Scheherazade in the back of his cab. They arrived in the elegant crescent and the driver dropped them at their front door. Lucinda had elbowed Rob in the ribs to wake him up and as a preliminary warning of further punishment to come.

"Come on honey. It was just silly boys talk. I certainly don't want to spend any time or money with some dodgy foreign prostitute. Why would I when I've got you?" Rob leant forward to kiss Lucinda but she moved out of range and his lips met fresh air.

"If you want a Russian then you go find one." Lucinda struggled to remove her costume.

"I don't want a Russian," said Rob in a whining voice that was laced with too much strong drink. "I-just-want-you."

"Right then." said Lucinda dropping the last of her outfit on to the floor and wrapping her towelling dressing gown around her before marching out of the bedroom.

Rob must have fallen asleep on the bed face down because when he woke he was still half dressed as an Arab. He tried to sit up but found that his wrists had been strapped to the bed head. For a moment he thought he was dreaming.

"What the…." he said and in the half light he could just make out the shape of a woman approaching the bed side wearing what looked like a Cossack's fur hat and as far as he could tell nothing else.

"So Comrade," said a husky foreign sounding voice. "You want to full around wiz a Russian yes no?"

166

"Yes. No." said Rob feebly.

"Furst you drink." said the female voice. Rob thought that was the last thing he needed to do unless it was a glass of water.

"Wodka," said his tormentor and from out of nowhere a clear bottle of strong white spirit was poured all over the writhing Arab's back.

"Luce. What the fuck are you doing?" shouted Rob.

"My name is Olga," said Lucinda, "And you've been a naughty boy. The KGB don't like naughty boys so ve haf ways to punish you. Yes No."

"Come on Luce. I'm bloody soaked. Please untie me?" Rob was beginning to sound desperate.

"Six lashes is demanded," said Lucinda and she conjured up a bamboo stick, the sort used to support climbing plants in a garden.

"Come on love." said Rob just as the first of six well aimed lashes struck him across his thinly covered bottom.

"Owwww! Bloody hell!" he shouted more with shock than pain. His protest had no effect. The six pathetic strokes were taken badly but given with the sort of pleasure that Lucinda found very stimulating. Having delivered her last she dropped the cane on the floor and spread herself naked on top of her lightly beaten husband.

"That didn't really hurt, did it darlink?" she whispered in his ear.

"Not one bit," said Rob. "So please undo these silly ties and let me up."

"Only if you promise to make love to me," she whispered.

"I promise I will but it'll hurt you more than it hurts me."

"That sounds vulgar," said Lucinda in his ear as she leant over to undo the restraints.

"You better believe it," said Rob and he turned to face his aroused and naked wife, the rabbit fur hat still in place on her pretty head.

"It's up the Volga for you tonight, comrade."

Well … Sheherazade … is that Luce's attempt at a joke?
Makes me wince at my last effort to seduce Miles. I wonder what
kind of mood he'll be in when he gets home tonight. We need
to talk.

11.30 pm
Miles came home from work tired and irritable. He phoned the
insurance company and they have offered to pay for a driver until
the consultant gives him the all clear. He's no happier though.
I made his favourite meal, chicken jalfrezi, easy for him to eat
one-handedly. He poked about at his plate and finally pushed it
aside, hardly touched.

"What's wrong Miles?"
"What's not wrong, Beth?" He sounded weary.
"Please talk to me. Is it the paintings that's upsetting you? You
haven't even mentioned what you thought of them."
"Do you really want to know?"
"Of course."
"Okay. I thought they were embarrassing, distasteful and
frankly, pornographic."
I was shocked by his response.
"I see."
"How can I compete with Laurent, tell me that?"
"What do you mean, compete? There's no competition. He's
not even on the agenda."
"No? He still thinks he can give you what you want. Kids, a
fancy lifestyle. House in the South of France. You're his muse, his
raison d'être, he said."
"I don't understand you Miles."
'It's quite obvious that he's still in love with you and while
he has those paintings, I don't think I can ever make love to

168

you again without seeing you sprawled over that sofa with your pregnant belly."

This came as a shock. I didn't know what to say. He took my hand across the table and I could see tears in his eyes.

Miles continued, "I'm not proud of the way I feel Beth. When I saw the portraits, I just felt so jealous of your life with Laurent, knowing he had that knowledge of your body, every intimate part of you. I feel you don't belong to me anymore. Seeing the love in your eyes and that deep connection you had with him and the baby. I just can't compete with that, I'm sorry."

"But Miles, that was a long time ago. Laurent means nothing to me now. Yes, I was upset at losing the baby and yes, if I'm honest, I do feel very broody after seeing the portraits but I love you Miles. I want to be with you, don't shut me out."

"I need time Beth. I need to sort things out in my head. I don't want kids, and I thought you didn't either but when I saw you in that painting with the baby, I realised how cruel it is to deprive you of that. I don't know if I can give you that Beth. Maybe you would be better off with someone else."

"I don't want anyone else Miles. I think you've allowed Laurent to colour your vision." I decided to come clean. "I should really tell you that after we had dinner that night in London, he took me to see the paintings in a lock up and tried his best to seduce me."

"A lock-up, Beth! And I suppose you expect me to believe nothing happened! How many more lies?"

I was trying to be honest with him but I'd just made things worse. And then I got angry and said stupid things.

"Yeah, like nothing happened between you and Shonagh! You can believe all you like Miles, but whichever way you look at it,

169

Laurent and I share the loss of our baby. That's something that will always be between us."

He grasped me hard by the arms and looked straight into my eyes.

"Be honest for once Beth. Do you really want to have another baby?"

"Yes Miles, I do." There. I'd said it.

He let go, turned his back and walked into the bedroom. He took a hold-all from the cupboard and starting packing some clothes.

"What are you doing?"

"I'm leaving. I need space to think."

"You can't leave me Miles. Please don't go. You're breaking my heart."

"I'm sorry Beth, but I don't know you anymore. Maybe in time I'll understand but for now I think it's best for both of us if we don't see each other for a while."

He'd made up his mind. I could see that.

"Where will you stay?"

"I don't know, maybe a Travelodge or something."

"That's stupid. I'll move out. I can go to Imo's"

"I don't see why you should move out. It's my problem."

"No Miles, it's *our* problem and I'm the cause of it. I'll leave tomorrow. You can sleep in the spare room tonight."

I couldn't believe I was saying these things. I felt like a robot with no feelings, like it was all a bad dream. But it's not. Miles is asleep in the spare room and I'm crying myself to death. Damn Laurent and damn his paintings!

But Miles is right. All this has changed me. I don't know what I want any more. Maybe I should go back to Uzes, meet my demons and face up to the grief. And maybe then I'll be able to forgive myself. And perhaps Miles will forgive me too. I love him so much.